# The Midnight Heiress

ONCE UPON A REGENCY

# ASHTYN NEWBOLD

ISBN 13: 9781092618328

Editing by Tori MacArthur
Cover design by Amanda Conley

# Chapter 1

Turning his back on Thornwall was the most difficult thing Aiden Notley had ever done. And he had endured many difficult things. As he trailed behind his stepfather and two stepbrothers, he set his jaw and tightened his grip on his trunk, willing himself to keep his gaze fixed on the carriage ahead. To look back at his childhood home now would only make it harder to leave behind. It was the memories of his parents—the smiles, the laughter, the kindness, and the loving words—that made his departure so difficult.

Unlike the house, those memories were things life could never take from him, no matter how greedy it became.

"Aiden! Step to it, boy." His stepfather, the Marquess of Aveley, stood impatiently at the door of his carriage. His own trunk lay at his feet, waiting for the ever-willing hands of Aiden to strap it onto the back

1

of the conveyance. Lord Aveley's two sons, who had already entered the carriage, leaned against their respective cushions with smirks on both their faces.

Since Lord Aveley had decided to sell Thornwall six months before, he had dismissed the entire household staff, some of which were Aiden's dearest friends. Aiden should have known he would be left to fill the role of every servant. He was butler, housekeeper, footman, cook, and valet. A man-of-all-work. To Lord Aveley, who received very few visitors that might scorn the practice, there was nothing amiss with such a set-up.

Aiden would have never complied if not for his lack of university education. He could not afford an education, nor was he given a scholarship. He could not enter a respectable profession in medicine, military, or the clergy without a formal education. So a tradesman he would become. Until then, he needed a place to live, and in exchange for his stepfather's generosity, he was required to work as an omnipresent servant in his home. Without wages.

Aiden stooped over at the waist and hoisted his stepfather's traveling trunk onto the back of the carriage, strapping it up tightly. His stepbrothers, Miles, the Earl of Orsett, and Lord Evan Browning, had also deposited their trunks on the ground behind the back wheels of the carriage, assuming Aiden would strap them up.

After securing his stepfather's trunk, he hoisted up Evan's, grunting with the effort. The weight felt as if he had packed his trunk with solid gold. But Aiden knew it could not be true. Most of Lord Aveley's motivation to sell Thornwall and dismiss his staff was to alleviate his financial burden. His sons had little to expect by way of fortune upon his death.

Little to nothing.

Soon after Aiden's mother died, Lord Aveley had abandoned all reason. He had foolishly given his daughter an immense dowry to marry her off to a viscount, further depleting his funds. He had then proceeded to gamble away several thousand pounds. His eldest son, Miles, would one day be the Marquess of Aveley, but with little wealth and property behind the name. And Evan, indolent as he was, preferred the thought of marrying into wealth of his own rather than seek a profession.

Knowing his own fate as a tradesman, Aiden had hope of one day becoming a cordwainer through apprenticeship, constructing the sort of shoes his mother loved. As a young boy, his mother and father had often danced in the drawing room, his mother often declaring that a lady's shoes determined her dancing ability. The more becoming, flexible, and lovely the shoe, the more confident the lady. And the more confident the lady, the more regal. The more regal, the more graceful.

Aiden had never suspected shoes to mean so much, but if they were valued by his mother, then they must be important. If there were ever a way to honor her, it would be to construct shoes that would produce smiles like the ones she wore while trying on a new pair.

"Gads, I've seen tortoises that move faster than Aiden Notley." The snide voice of Miles came muffled through the carriage door. "Father, please do remind me why we haven't yet sent the simpleton packing."

A wave of snickering came from Evan. Aiden had always thought Evan possessed a strangely high-pitched voice and laugh for a man. Even for a woman. "I do like to see him serve us," Evan said. "Think of how dull life would be if we couldn't watch him struggle with the weight of our trunks."

Aiden bit the inside of his cheek, thrusting Miles's trunk atop the carriage with great force, setting the entire vehicle swaying. An angry grunt sounded from within, a clear sign of annoyance. It came, no doubt, from his stepfather. Aiden knew the sound well.

Tying the last of the straps, Aiden pulled the carriage door open, meeting the stern gaze of his stepfather, who lounged against his seat. His dark eyes surveyed Aiden with unexplained malice. "What do you suppose you are doing? You'll be riding on the back, of course."

Aiden didn't protest. He would rather ride in the open air with the sun upon his face than endure several hours of spiteful remarks and irritating laughter from his stepbrothers. Without a word, he closed the carriage door, walking around the back to find a place among the various traveling trunks and bags. As he be-

4

gan to hoist himself up, he heard the brisk command of Lord Aveley to the coachman, setting the team of horses into abrupt motion.

Aiden jerked back with the sudden movement, losing his grip on the back of the carriage. He fell hard to the gravel, the impact stealing his breath for several seconds. Pain shot through his arms and legs where tiny rocks had scraped him. He rolled over, rubbing bits of gravel from his skin, blowing dust from his face. The carriage came to a stop several feet ahead, a mixture of deep and high-pitched laughter floating up through the air like the dust all around him.

He struggled to his feet before pressing the hem of his torn shirt against a cut on his wrist, the white fabric quickly turning red with his blood. The carriage window opened, revealing the mirthful expression of Evan. His dark hair and eyes contrasted sharply with his extremely white skin, the white of his teeth blending almost seamlessly with his complexion. "Oh, stepbrother, did you take a fall? Father offers his sincere apology."

The deep chuckling from within belied his statement.

Aiden took a deep breath, setting his jaw and wiping the dust from his forehead as he approached the back of the carriage. In one swift motion, he lifted himself onto the seat, attaining a firm grip before his stepfather could try to derail him again.

"Are you secure on the carriage? We should hate to see you fall again."

Aiden ignored the snide comments as he always did, trying also to ignore the pain that inched over his palms and wrist. He heard the click of the window as it closed, leaving him to the much more pleasant sounds of nature. The flick of the reins met his ears as the carriage came to a much more gradual start, the large wheels crackling against the gravel beneath him.

Melancholy reverberated in his chest as he watched Thornwall grow smaller in the distance. He memorized the landscape of the front property, the bushes and trees and neat grass he had taken great care to keep up over the last six months. He envisioned the many friends his mother and father had invited for dinner parties and soirees, how they had smiled as they ascended the steps, sharing Aiden's love for Mr. and Mrs. Notley and for Thornwall.

The home had been his mother's, a property she had purchased with the large inheritance that had come unexpectedly from her grandmother. A year after Aiden's father's death, the property had become a burden for her to manage alone. Lord Aveley had come with the appearance of grace and kindness, offering his hand in marriage. Stunned and grateful, she had accepted. In their marriage settlement, Thornwall and all its properties had been passed to Lord Aveley. Not until her unexpected fever and death two short years later did the marquess reveal his true character. It had broken Aiden's heart to see his parents' possessions sold to pay Lord Aveley's debts. Aiden had managed to hide a pair of slippers that belonged to his mother and a pocket watch of his father's before the auction had claimed the rest.

He exhaled his sorrow, breathing in the bright summer air. There was no sense in longing for the past. It was gone, buried with his mother and father and the joy they had shared. But it was not that Aiden was without joy, not at all. Without the prominent joy of a loving family, and a warm, comfortable home, he had learned to find joy in the smaller things of life. He appreciated and noticed things he never had before. Every kind word he ever received now felt like a precious gift. Every smile that did not contain spite or mockery, he clung to. Each sunset gave him hope for tomorrow, and each sunrise gave him strength to continue on. He counted the stars at night, taking note of their majesty, knowing his parents now lived among them.

He tipped his head against the back of the carriage, vibrations coursing through his skull. The heat of the sun beat down on his face as he closed his eyes. He would be riding on the back of the carriage for two days on the long journey to Lord Aveley's last remaining property, a smaller home called Colborne Hall, located in Gravesend, an area of England containing hills, marshes, lush woods, and distant mountains. His stepfather had described the place in few details, as he had only visited his property there once.

Aiden groaned at the thought of all the refurbishments that would need to take place upon their arrival, and that the responsibility would fall solely to him. He could scarcely imagine the quantities of dust and grime that would likely coat the furnishings, and the ghastly status of the landscape. But his mother had always taught him to look for the good in every situation.

At least he would have much to keep him busy upon their arrival at Colborne Hall.

\* \* \*

The following two days were filled with sweat and dust and aching muscles. Lord Aveley lacked the funds and the compassion to purchase a room at the inn for Aiden, leaving him to sleep within the carriage. By the time they reached Gravesend the next afternoon, Aiden's face was coated in dirt and sweat, his back throbbed with pain, and his face was severely sunburnt.

At least the cuts on his hands and arms had begun to heal.

Gravesend was very different than he had imagined it would be. Located on higher ground, the town had several hills of vibrant green. As the carriage passed through the center of the town, Aiden surveyed the rustic shops, taking note of a cordwainer establishment among them. He caught a quick glimpse of a pair of intricate slippers in the window. They reminded him of his mother's favorite pair. He memorized the location of the shop. He would come back at his first opportunity to inquire about the possibility of an apprenticeship.

As the carriage carried him past the town center, a cloud passed over the sun, relieving Aiden of the relentless summer heat for a brief moment. From what he had seen thus far, the houses of Gravesend appeared rather small, built closely to one another, the rooftops sloping down and nearly touching on both sides. In the distance, a massive estate loomed on a hill, the gray stone appearing darker under the clouded sky. Could it be Colborne Hall? He couldn't imagine keeping up with such expansive property on his own.

He squinted, noticing the neat grounds. Relief poured through him. It could not be the deserted estate they were to inhabit. But even if Colborne Hall were half the size, it would be extremely difficult to manage on his own. If his stepfather hoped to entertain guests at their new property, he would have to employ more staff. There was no way Aiden could do it all, and it would hinder Lord Aveley's reputation if it was discovered he only had one servant—an unpaid servant who was also his stepson.

The carriage crossed the road in front of the looming estate, giving Aiden a closer view of the structure. The road crossed behind the estate, passing through the nearby woods. Less than a mile away, a slightly smaller house appeared. With golden brown stone,

multiple dirt streaked windows, and overgrown vege-
tation, Aiden determined that this had to be Colborne
Hall.

As he suspected, the carriage pulled up to the drive,
coming to an abrupt halt. Aiden jumped down from
his seat, stretching his legs and wiping the perspiration from his brow. He studied the tangled, overgrown
grass and the weeds that sprouted among it. Bushes
stretched high near the front doors with vines climbing over the stone. There was much work to be done
outside.

Lord Aveley descended from the carriage, filling
his lungs with the crisp air of Gravesend. "One would
expect a marquess to live in greater grandeur than
this." He grimaced, his narrowed eyes appraising the
property. He turned to Aiden. "I expect this estate to
be suitable for guests within a fortnight." His eyes
widened momentarily as he took in Aiden's disheveled
appearance. "And *you* will not be in attendance if any
guests come to call."

A fortnight? It would take much longer than that to
preen the front property into something presentable,
and Aiden hadn't even seen the condition of the back
property and the interior of the house. He cleared his
throat. "I do not think it possible to make this property presentable in such a short time. Do you plan to hire
servants?"

Lord Aveley squared his shoulders. "I will solicit
for servants around town, but until then, you will do

nothing else until this house is fit for a marquess and his esteemed guests." Lord Aveley fixed Aiden with a scowl. "And you are not to introduce yourself as any relation of mine. We are in a new part of the country. If you are questioned, do not claim any association with me or with Miles and Evan. Do you understand? If your residence is questioned, then you are to declare yourself a servant in this home, nothing more."

Aiden nodded, more than glad to accept such terms. He would rather keep a familial distance between himself and his stepfather and stepbrothers. Aiden's only true family was dead.

"The rest of our possessions should be arriving within the week," Lord Aveley said. "You are to bring them into the house and arrange them as they were in Thornwall."

Aiden nodded again, following behind his stepfather and stepbrothers as they moved toward the house. The interior was just as Aiden had suspected: in complete disarray. The wallpaper had peeled in many places, with water fading the patterns and giving the home a musky scent. The marble floors were coated with dust, as were all the furnishings of the entry hall. Lord Aveley pulled on a sheet that covered a portrait, grimacing at the man depicted in the painting.

"My grandfather," Lord Aveley said with disgust. "You must replace this with my portrait as soon as it arrives. You may flank it with portraits of Miles and Evan, and one of Arabella as well."

"As you wish." Aiden turned toward the nearest door, opening it to reveal the drawing room. The furniture had been draped with sheets, lessening the dust that would otherwise have gathered in the creases of the cushions. He would need to acquaint himself with the kitchen first, and make it his first priority. Lord Aveley would want a nice meal this evening, and Aiden would be responsible for preparing it.

Miles and Evan climbed the wide staircase, disappearing down the second floor hall. Dismayed grumbles carried down to the first floor, and Evan returned to the top of the staircase. "Aiden! I will need my room prepared immediately. I wish to rest but the bed is filthy." He rubbed his fingers together, staring at the dirt between them with disgust. "I will need the cobwebs cleared from the doorway as well."

For a moment Aiden entertained the idea of capturing a few spiders and planting them among Evan's blankets.

*Be kind.* His mother's cajoling statement entered his thoughts. She had used it on him often as a boy, affirming the importance of kindness in all circumstances. *The kind person is the happiest person*, she had often said. *The happiest person is the one that gives more than he takes, loves more than he hates, and builds more than he breaks.* Aiden had learned through living with his stepfamily that giving, loving, and building those that take, hate, and break was more difficult than anything he had ever done. His mother

12

would claim that those sort of people were most in need of kindness.

And so Aiden would prepare Evan's room. He would do so without complaint. He would prepare dinner and tame the grounds and dust the furnishings. He would do it for his mother, if only to assure him that she smiled down upon his efforts.

Aiden often dreamed of the day he would escape Lord Aveley's influence. Life in Gravesend could be his opportunity. He thought of the cordwainer's shop he had seen on their drive. When he went to the market to purchase the needed food for dinner, he would inquire about an apprenticeship.

# Chapter 2

Lady Katherine Golding, the eldest and only child of the Duke of Chatham, rested her head in her hands, enjoying the warmth of the sun on the back of her neck. She lifted her gaze to the gardens before her. Leaves rustled in the light summer breeze, and she listened to the soft sounds contentedly. The sounds intensified into something loud and crunching.

Footfalls.

Her stomach sunk to her knees at the sight of Mr. Boyle, skittering through the flowers and bushes like a mouse evading a cat as he approached her. It wasn't just Mr. Boyle's actions that resembled a mouse, but his appearance as well. He was quite small—at least three inches shorter than Katherine but not nearly as narrow. He had small, dark eyes and a set of prominent teeth, which grinned up at her as he made his bows.

"Lady Katherine, how do you do?" His voice, little more than a squeak, became lost in the summer breeze that surrounded them.

She gave a polite smile from her place on the bench. Mr. Boyle never failed to invite himself onto the Chatham property, sneaking through the gardens as if he knew he was not welcome there.

"I am quite well, Mr. Boyle." Kate scolded herself for coming to her favorite place in the gardens today. She should have known Mr. Boyle would find her there. He had found her there the day before. And the day before that. "What brings you to Silverbard, sir?" Her voice came out more exasperated than she intended, but she could not help it. Mr. Boyle had expressed his interest in courting her twice now, though he was at least twice her age. She did not know what else she could do to deter his attention. He was proving even more difficult to get rid of than the last insincere suitor that had come calling.

More difficult than the last ten, in fact.

Kate's father had sent her to London the previous season, making society aware of the immense dowry tied to her name. Thirty thousand pounds was enough to draw a multitude of eligible men, yet Kate had still returned from London unattached. Much to her father's dismay, she had not found a man she could ever love. She knew they were not interested in her heart— only her wealth. When word had spread around her home town of Sheffield of her dowry, and her father

15

had successfully eliminated the entailment of his secondary properties, willing one of his largest estates to her, a whole new array of fortune-hunting suitors had begun their pursuit. It was, in a word, exhausting.

"'Tis such a lovely estate, my lady. How interesting that you should be in possession of an estate called *Silver*bard when your surname is indeed, *Gold*ing. Yet you are more handsome and desirable than silver or gold." Mr. Boyle's beady eyes squinted in a smile, the sunlight beating down on his graying hair.

Kate pressed her lips together to keep from laughing at his attempt at flattery. She knew his words to be a complete lie. "You are too kind. You must stop or I shall begin thinking myself equivalent to a diamond."

Mr. Boyle's eyes widened, a ring of white surrounding the dark irises. "The most beautiful diamond in all of the world. Never have I beheld such lovely hair. 'Tis the color of freshly baked bread, and your eyes are the color of emerald. Well, slightly lighter than emerald; perhaps an emerald that has been resting in the sunlight. It is a lovely sight when paired with your complexion. Many a freckle can be overcome by a set of enchanting eyes and a mane of shining hair." Mr. Boyle extended his hand, his shaking, heavy-knuckled fingers coming toward her head.

Kate ducked away, standing abruptly from her place on the bench before Mr. Boyle could touch her hair. Why had she thought it wise to leave her bonnet inside?

Mr. Boyle retracted his paw, his front teeth slipping over his lower lip. "Ah. I suspect you wish to take a turn around the gardens with me?"

"Pardon me?" Kate couldn't imagine how the man would view her abrupt standing as a subtle hint that she wanted to walk with him.

He gave a little laugh—a sound very nearly a giggle—before extending his arm to her. "I shall never tire of seeing the exquisite gardens of Silverbard." He stared pointedly at his elbow when she hesitated to take it.

She released a quiet sigh of exasperation, casting her eyes downward as she rested her fingers lightly on his arm. To decline would be incredibly rude, and she was exhausted from her efforts to evade him.

"Of course, the gardens are made even more exquisite by your habitation of them, my lady." He bared his teeth in a semblance of a smile.

She watched her feet as she walked, attempting to steer Mr. Boyle toward the back door of the house where she could make a hasty escape. As they passed a hedge near the door, a deep growling sounded from within before the furry head of her Skye Terrier, Freddy, came bursting through the dense leaves.

"Oh!" Mr. Boyle stumbled backward, tripping over a prominent root in the grass, which sent him sprawling onto the ground. Freddy leapt from the bushes, growling with renewed vigor. He leapt onto Mr. Boyle's belly and offered his fiercest bark before jumping down. Mr. Boyle's ample belly provided a nice spring to Freddy's dismount.

Kate covered her mouth to hide the laughter that threatened to burst out of her composed expression. She scooped Freddy into her arms, holding his little head to her chest. He panted, stretching his neck to lick her cheek.

"Sir, I am so very sorry for my dog's behavior." Kate backed away from Mr. Boyle as he stood, anger fuming in his dark eyes.

"That is the most dreadful creature I have ever encountered!" He thrust his finger toward Freddy. When he noticed Kate's look of dismay, he corrected his disheveled expression. "Er—well, I suppose it is not the *most* dreadful. I rather like the creature. It seems a lively sort of animal, very... energetic. Yes, *energetic* is the word I meant to say."

Kate gave her most pleasant smile as she stroked Freddy's thick gray fur. "He is my dearest friend, you know. He will always be my most treasured companion. I will never part with him."

Mr. Boyle swallowed, pushing back the hair from his forehead that had become soaked with perspiration. "Never, my lady?"

"Never. Not now, not when I am married, not until the day little Freddy passes on, a day I wish not to dwell upon."

Mr. Boyle nodded, a spark of motivation entering his eyes. "Do you envision yourself marrying soon?"

Kate bit her tongue. Why had she mentioned marriage in the presence of this man? He would take every word on the subject as encouragement. If only she could convince him that her dowry came on the condition of her marriage to a man below the age of forty, then perhaps he would leave her be. "Oh, Mr. Boyle. I have only recently made my bows in society. I am a mere eighteen years old."

"Well, I daresay it is much better to marry now than become a spinster."

Kate's skin bristled with annoyance. She shifted Freddy to one arm, propping him on her hip. "I must be going now, Mr. Boyle."

"So very soon? I only just arrived."

*Precisely.*

"I'm afraid I took ill last week and have yet to recover." She feigned a sneeze, burying it in the fur of her dog.

Mr. Boyle gasped. "I suspect you have an allergy to the little creature! For your own health, you must rid yourself of him." He stumbled forward with outstretched arms, as if he meant to assist her in *ridding* herself of Freddy.

She skirted away. "I will never do that. For a dog makes a much better companion than a man." Turning on her heel, she gave a resolute nod. "Good day, sir."

He gave a huffed breath in response before stammering a quick, "Good day."

Kate pushed through the back door, setting Freddy

on the floor. He scampered away, his little claws clicking on the marble. She straightened her posture, drawing a breath deep into her lungs. How could she feel so stifled and trapped within such expansive walls?

Silverbard was the largest estate in the county, home of her father, the Duke of Chatham. Four stories tall with endless throngs of servants and property that stretched deep within the neighboring woods, it would never be described by anyone but herself as *stifling*. Her family also owned two other estates, one in Gravesend and one in Nottingham. Kate had never been to either, but she often dreamed of escaping Silverbard to one of the other estates, starting over in a new area of England where her inheritance was unknown. As her circumstances were at present, she could never trust any man's intentions to marry her.

Her mother, Lady Chatham, swept around the corner, a bright smile on her cheeks. "Katherine, my dear. Did I just see Mr. Boyle out the window?"

She swallowed, praying that her mother hadn't witnessed Freddy's attack on the man. "Indeed. But I sent him on his way."

Her mother's eyes rounded. "You… sent him on his way? How exactly did you do that?"

Kate cursed her tongue for claiming responsibility for Mr. Boyle's departure. "He did not enjoy Freddy's company and so… well, I explained in the most polite terms possible, I assure you, that I prefer Freddy's company over his own, so it would be best if he left us."

20

Her mother gasped. "Katherine!"

She wished she were still holding Freddy, so she could bury her face in his fur and avoid the disapproving stare of her mother.

"You cannot deter every suitor that comes calling."

"And why not?" Kate felt her cheeks flushing. "You have said how greatly you detest fortune hunters. That is all these men are. They do not care for me and they never shall. All they care for is wealth and property. By marrying me they will be in possession of the largest allotment of land in the county. They will gain a quick thirty thousand pounds to their accounts as well."

A sadness entered her mother's eyes, a weight that Kate rarely saw. "One day a man will see *you* as the greatest prize."

Kate shook her head. "How could he? Gold shines much brighter than I do."

Her mother struggled for a response, but Kate didn't need reassurance. She needed sympathy and understanding. She did not wish to be such a sought-after heiress. She did not wish to manage such large property. All she needed to be happy one day was true love, a comfortable living, and a dog on her lap. She did not wish for anything more.

"How is Papa faring?" Kate asked, happy to change the subject.

Her mother's posture relaxed, as if discussing her husband's declining health was a more pleasant topic than her daughter's fortune. "He is well enough. He is bored, that is all. He has little to occupy his thoughts and time. The physician said he will likely survive this bout of illness just as he did the last time."

An idea struck Kate. "Do you suppose Papa would like an excursion? To Gravesend, perhaps? I know he does not prefer his property there, but he has not been in years. I did hear the tenants have departed for the summer."

Her mother pinched her lips together in thought. "I will speak with him on the matter. But I doubt he will be interested in leaving the comfort of Silverbard at this time."

"Even if it will bring great joy to his daughter?"

Her mother raised one eyebrow. "And why would it bring you such great joy?"

Kate smiled, her thoughts running wild. "The people of Gravesend do not know of my dowry. If perchance there are any eligible men among the town, I will have an opportunity to socialize among them without sharing any knowledge of my inheritance. That way I may decipher if any man could hold true feelings for me."

Straightening the pendant at her neck, Kate's mother frowned. "We cannot possibly keep it a secret forever. And why should we? Your dowry and property will attract many wonderful suitors."

"Such as Mr. Boyle?" Kate grimaced. "We must keep it a secret if we go, at least for a time. For my sake, please say you'll try."

"Kate—" Her mother closed her mouth, as if re-considering her words. "Any man of sense will like to know what your financial situation is before beginning a courtship."

"Then we… fabricate something?"

"Katherine!"

She bit her lower lip. "Very well, but we do not need to speak of it in such clear terms. There is no need for every man in Gravesend to know that I am an heiress of such proportions. That information ought only to be revealed in a marriage settlement between my suitor and Papa."

Her mother heaved a sigh, the exhalation sending her neat curls to feather on her forehead. "I am fairly certain your father will not approve of the venture, but I will inquire nonetheless."

Hope sprung within Kate, growing stronger by the second. "Thank you, Mama."

* * *

Kate could hardly sleep in anticipation of her father's response. Her mother had spoken with him and he had been rather indecisive on the matter. When Kate paid him a visit in his rooms the next day, however, he met her with an encouraging smile.

"Come in, my dear." He was sitting up today, in a chair by the window. Her father had bouts of severe illness almost every year. It usually cleared by spring, but this year had been an exception. His coughing and discomfort had persisted through the melting of the snow, the blooming of the trees, and the enduring warmth of summer.

"I have reached a decision pertaining to your request." His light eyes twinkled merrily. "Gravesend seems like a very welcome diversion. The change of scenery will do well to raise my spirits, and it will be even better to see you happy."

Kate hadn't expected such a ready response.

"I have heard that the Marquess of Aveley and his sons will be removing to Gravesend as well. His eldest, Lord Orsett, would be an excellent choice for you. I will ensure you are introduced upon our arrival."

Kate's heart sank.

"Lord Orsett will be drawn to your dowry, to be sure," her father continued. "The younger son would be the less desirable choice, but he is also well respected. He will be in great need of marrying well, for he does not have property or fortune to inherit, but his connections are very agreeable. I daresay a match with either man would be admirable."

Kate wrung her hands together, attempting to hide the disappointment on her face. "Do you suppose we might... keep my inheritance and dowry a secret upon our arrival?"

Her father's eyes widened. "Oh, no, of course not. I already wrote to Lord Aveley concerning our arrival and my desire to have you introduced to his sons. They know of your sizeable inheritance."

Kate took a step back. "Papa, please do not tell anyone else. I do not wish for a new swarm of suitors."

He chuckled, a low and rattling sound. "How droll you are, Kate. Any woman in your position would be quite flattered to have so many suitors."

"Not if they are in similitude to Mr. Boyle, and not if they only desire my fortune." Her voice came out dull and quiet.

"Oh, Kate. I am certain one of these men will see you for the amiable and beautiful young woman that you are."

Kate didn't bother arguing with him. She cast her eyes down, her throat burning with tears of disappointment. She held them in.

Her father sighed, apparently sensing her dejection. "I am sorry, my dear. I know you do not like the attention, but your season in London did not get you any offer of marriage. The dowry is the most reliable way to draw suitors to you. I want to ensure you have a man to assist in managing Silverbard."

"I understand, Papa." Kate tried to brighten her voice. "At least it is just Lord Aveley and his sons that know of my dowry."

Her father chuckled. "Yes, for now. Gossip spreads like fire in Gravesend. If nothing else, it will bring respect to our family. There is nothing to worry yourself over. We shall depart within the week. The servants are already busy preparing our trunks."

Kate nodded and thanked him before trudging from the room. Her boots felt as if they had doubled in weight since entering her father's bedchamber. All she had to look forward to was another multitude of Mr. Boyles. She could only hope that Gravesend had more to offer than that.

# Chapter 3

By the end of his first week in Gravesend, Aiden had yet to find the opportunity to speak with the cordwainer in town. He had been to the market twice to make purchases for Lord Aveley, but had found the cordwainer busy with customers.

The property was far from being ready for guests, and Aiden had been working without rest for the entire week. He had managed to tame the kitchen and front property, but the other rooms of the house were still covered in dust. Lord Aveley wanted every piece of silver and every sconce polished, as well as the floor of the ballroom. Aiden was also required to feed the animals, cook for Lord Aveley and his sons, and assist them in their daily tasks. Aiden persisted and survived on the knowledge that one day he would be free of such responsibility. He would become a cordwainer, rent his own small house, and live in peace.

"Aiden!" Evan called, appearing above the staircase with a monstrously tied cravat. "Come tie this for me. I cannot do it myself." He scowled down at the knot he had made.

Aiden set down the cloth he had been using to clear a spot of grime from the entry hall floor. He stood, his back aching. When he reached the top of the staircase, Evan dropped his hands, allowing Aiden to fix his cravat.

"It must be perfect," he said, his chin turned upward.

Aiden felt one of his eyebrows raise. "Why do you require a perfect cravat today of all days?"

"The Heiress of Silverbard has arrived."

"Heiress?" Aiden tugged on the fabric, twisting it into the shape he had been forced to perfect.

Evan rolled his eyes, as if Aiden should have been fully aware of this woman's arrival. "Her father is the Duke of Chatham. She is to inherit his largest estate and has a sizeable dowry as well." His eyes lit up like a predator approaching a helpless kill. "Her father would like her to become acquainted with Miles and me. I must be prepared to meet the family should I encounter them in town."

Aiden finished the knot. "How fortunate for you."

"Do not be so envious." Evan grinned, touching a hand to his cravat with a pompous smile.

"I am not envious."

Evan clicked his tongue. "And there is no need to be so defensive. Now go. Finish cleaning."

Aiden turned around, making his way back down the stairs. When he was certain Evan had returned to the company of his looking glass, Aiden slipped out the front door. The sun was hot today, but his sunburnt skin had healed, leaving it a shade tanner than before, and several shades darker than his porcelain stepbrothers.

On his walk to the cordwainer's shop he entertained himself with thoughts of Miles and Evan and how they would react if their skin was to be darkened by the sun. Aiden wouldn't be surprised if either of them would faint over the misfortune of having skin such an unfashionable color.

The walk took little time at all. He drew a deep breath before opening the door, half-expecting the cordwainer to be occupied with customers once again. Instead, he found an empty shop strewn with many tools and half-constructed shoes, bolts of fabric propped against the walls and rigid chairs positioned by the fire. The entire shop smelled of wood and age, the floorboards creaking as Aiden made his way to the counter. He recognized the man behind it as the cordwainer, though they had yet to meet. He had heard the man was called Mr. Haskett.

Aiden approached with a polite smile, offering a nod in greeting. "Mr. Haskett, is it?"

The man studied Aiden with speculation, likely assuming by his appearance he could not possibly be a customer come to purchase a fine pair of boots. His eyes peered out behind half-rimmed spectacles, his dark hair speckled in gray. "Indeed."

"I am Mr. Aiden Notley. I could not help but admire your workmanship from outside. I came to inquire after the possibility of an apprenticeship. I would love to learn from a man as skilled as yourself."

Mr. Haskett's eyes sparked with interest. "Just last week I would have refused, but we have a potentially profitable family that has just arrived in Gravesend. I suspect they will be in want of new shoes before the month is finished." He rubbed his jaw. "Business will certainly multiply. I could put another set of hands to use."

Aiden assumed the cordwainer spoke of the Duke and Duchess of Chatham and their daughter. Aiden pitied the young woman. She would soon be a source of competition between his stepbrothers. "I would be most grateful to be that set of hands," he said, returning his attention to the cordwainer.

Mr. Haskett hesitated for several seconds before nodding his approval. "You do seem the sort of man to work hard." He eyed the holes in Aiden's shirt and the knees of his trousers. "Where did you say you come from?"

"Colborne Hall. I am a servant in Lord Aveley's home."

Mr. Haskett's eyebrows rose. "The newly arrived marquess? Does he know of your pursuit of alternate employment? I can assure you I cannot pay an apprentice wages above what you are already earning in the home of a marquess."

Aiden shook his head. "He does not pay me."

Mr. Haskett's brow furrowed. "Are you an indentured servant of sorts?"

Aiden smiled. "Of sorts. But I aspire to be a cordwainer."

"And so you shall." Mr. Haskett smiled, extending his hand. "I hope you are prepared to work all hours of the night if necessary. You must report to my shop each morning at the rise of the sun if you are not still here from the previous day's work. There will be much to teach you."

With a firm nod, Aiden clutched Mr. Haskett's hand. "You may rely on me."

"I do not doubt it."

Momentarily pushing his other responsibilities from his mind, Aiden agreed to meet beginning the next morning.

As he exited the shop, his heart flooded with relief and hope. He kicked the dirt ahead of his feet as he walked, resisting the urge to jump in the air. Rather than taking the clear path back to Colborne Hall, he decided to take the longer route through the woods, if only to enjoy his time away from his stepfather and stepbrothers a moment longer. He picked at the edge of his shirt, studying the width of the holes in the fabric. His right sleeve had torn as well, appearing especially ragged under his old

31

waistcoat, as if he were a servant pretending to be a gentleman.

A sound to his left brought him to a halt on the wooded path. He leaned toward the sound, straining his ears. Had he imagined it?

"Freddy! Freddy! Come back here at once!" A firm female voice rose over the trees. Could it be a mother in search of her child? Aiden walked through the trees in the direction of the voice, intent to help in any way he could.

"Oh, Freddy." A sigh of relief met his ears. "You mustn't run off without your leash! I know you enjoy swimming very much but it is not safe! You could drown, you know."

Leash?

Aiden came out of the thicket where a shallow brook flowed, a fallen tree crossing over it. A young woman stood nimbly on the log, clutching a soaking ball of fur to her chest. It moved, revealing the small face of a dog, strings of long fur falling over its eyes. The young woman kissed its head, whispering something. The dog's ears twitched and it turned its nose up to her cheek. Its ears perked, eyes turning abruptly to Aiden, where he stood partially hidden behind a nearby tree. A surprisingly deep growl sounded from the animal, and his legs began thrashing with too much force to be constrained by the young lady.

She gasped in reprimand as the dog escaped her and landed with a splash in the brook. Her expression quickly transformed to fear when her dog did not resurface. "Freddy!" she half gasped, half shrieked. "Freddy?"

To Aiden's surprise, she jumped into the brook, the water reaching her knees, soaking through her fine skirts. Aiden rushed forward, hoping his abrupt arrival wouldn't frighten her. He caught sight of a patch of dark gray fur amid the murky water, then a small black nose, moving away with the current. He lunged forward and scooped the dog from the water, who emerged with bared teeth and strangled barking.

The young lady stood in the water with both hands covering her mouth, her eyes round with shock. Aiden gathered the dog into his arms, careful to evade the gnashing teeth as he calmed it, stroking its soaked head and scratching gently behind its ears. The dog's small body quickly relaxed, and it wriggled in his arms to face him. A set of brown eyes stared up at his face as the dog gained his footing on Aiden's arms and leapt up to lap the splashes of water off Aiden's cheek.

He laughed, regarding the dog for the sake of the young woman, who still stared at him in shock. "That is the proper way to thank your rescuer," he said, eyeing the dog with a smile. "For a moment when you tried to bite me I thought you a scoundrel."

Aiden lifted his eyes to the young woman, who had set to climbing out of the brook, her soaked skirts tangling around her feet. He shifted the dog to one arm, approaching her cautiously. "May I offer my assistance?"

She met his gaze briefly, the pale green of her eyes as unique as it was striking. "No, sir." She moved quickly, her movements suggesting that she was severely unsettled by his presence. It was not right for Aiden to be alone with her, but he had come across her by accident. He couldn't stand by and watch her struggle through the mud.

"Please, allow me to assist you." He extended his hand, which she ignored. Taking one large stride through the water, she let out a shriek as she tripped over her skirts, landing on her stomach half in and half out of the brook on the other side, mud splattering onto her face. She let out a huffed breath of frustration, her cheeks coloring to a becoming shade of pink.

Aiden offered his hand again, refraining from the laughter that surged in his chest. He had never seen such a resilient woman, one that would go to such great lengths to save her puppy, or one that would be so determined to deny the help of a man. She likely thought him to be a servant, far beneath her notice.

She glanced up at him from beneath a sheet of wet lashes, pushing herself to her feet without assistance and climbing out of the water on the opposite side of the brook. She arranged her skirts around her ankles, brushing bits of twigs and leaves from the now soiled ivory fabric. Her cheeks, splattered with mud, darkened yet another shade.

34

"Are you hurt?" Aiden asked.

She shook her head, her eyes flickering between him and her dog, still tucked beneath his arm.

"I wish I could have rescued you as I did your dog." He gave his most non-threatening smile, hoping to erase the look of terror and mortification on her face.

"It was not necessary." She wiped her palms on her skirts, cringing. "I would have rescued Freddy without any problem at all. We did not need your interference."

"My interference?" Aiden raised one eyebrow.

Her hair, previously pinned in crisp curls, hung dripping around her face. She pushed back a strand, clearing her throat. "But I—I thank you for your effort on his behalf."

"I fully believe you would have been capable." Aiden chuckled, scratching the dog behind his soaked ears. "But Freddy has already thanked me by agreeing not to bite me." He gripped the puppy around the middle, holding him out to get a good look. "Haven't you, Freddy? There will be no biting and scratching of your rescuer." The dog gave a friendly *yip* before resuming his squirming. Aiden laughed, glancing across the brook to the young woman. She watched him with a whisper of a smile on her lips, her sharp eyes intrigued. She quickly averted them, bringing a hand to her hair self-consciously.

"Are you a servant?" she asked, eyeing his clothing. She bit her lip, as if regretting the question.

Aiden nodded, obeying his stepfather's demand to claim no other title. "I am."

She looked down at her feet. Aiden knew as well as she did that they should not be conversing, given that they had not been introduced. But as their current circumstances demanded communication, he felt justified in it.

Something that resembled disappointment flashed in her eyes when she looked at him once again. "A household servant?"

He nodded. He did not need to explain that he was born into an upper class family, or that his stepfather was the Marquess of Aveley. Saying that he was a servant was not even a lie. He had been filling the role for so long now it was time he owned up to it.

Her eyes never left him, the color striking even from across the brook. "What may I call you?"

"My name is Aiden Notley." He smiled. "And what may I call you? Are you a servant as well?" He asked only in an effort to tease her, for he knew she couldn't possibly be a servant. She wore a dress of intricate detail, and she had ivory, unblemished skin. Even the way she held her head and posture revealed her elevated class.

She looked taken aback by the question, her eyes darting from side to side. He did not expect her to hesitate for so long before answering, but at least five seconds passed before she stumbled her response. "Yes, indeed, I am a servant."

He raised both eyebrows.

"I am a lady's maid." She swallowed. "My mistress asked that I exercise her dog while she went to tea. So you see how relieved I am that Freddy is safe. I would have fallen under great reprimand."

Aiden crossed his arms. He did not want to insult her by declaring her word to be false, but he didn't believe it at all. "I do not recall ever encountering a lady's maid wearing such… fine clothing."

"Oh, this?" She took a handful of the sullied skirts. "This is an old gown of my mistress's. She outgrew it and delivered it to me. I wear it when I go out, purely for the enjoyment of wearing such a beautiful thing."

Aiden narrowed his eyes slightly. Looking at her now, dirty and dripping, he could have believed she was a servant in disguise, but he had seen her before— he had glimpsed her pristine hair and clothing. Hadn't he? Or had he imagined it?

"Your voice," he said. "You do not speak as though you are a servant."

"Nor do you." She widened her gaze in a look of innocence. "I was not raised in such circumstances, but rather they fell upon me in recent years."

"I see." With her explanation, Aiden found her claim more convincing. He too had only become something of a servant in recent years. "I'm glad, then, that I was here to assist you with little Freddy." He turned the dog's face toward his, then pointed in the young lady's direction. "Mind your mistress."

A quiet laugh came from the young lady's maid. He looked up, hoping to catch a full smile on her face. The sight played on his heart like a pianoforte, vibrating and lovely. She had a beautiful smile.

"And what may I call you?" Aiden asked her, the tug of a smile on his own lips. "If I hope to train Freddy into compliance I must give him your name."

Her smile grew wider, a certain shyness to it. "You may call me... Miss Kate."

"Miss Kate." He leaned close to the dog's ear. "Mind Miss Kate, or I will hear of it and send you right back to the brook."

She gasped before falling into laughter. "You might think of an alternative punishment. Freddy seemed to quite like the water."

Aiden laughed, careful not to make his laugh too loud, to ensure he could still listen to the lovely sound of hers. "Indeed, he did. But punishment is not nearly as effective as rewards. The only reward that ever forces my dogs into submission is food. Perhaps I will bring him some meat if he behaves."

Miss Kate's laughter stopped. "You have dogs as well?"

"I do. But they do not have names nearly as refined as Freddy here."

She took a step closer to the water, her eyes sparking with interest. "What are their names?"

Aiden grinned. "Wrinkles, my Pug, and Puff, my Pomeranian."

"Wrinkles and Puff?" A look of sheer delight crossed her expression. "How charming." She looked down at her hands. "Do you suppose Wrinkles and Puff would like to meet Freddy? I might convince my mistress to allow me to take Freddy for another jaunt tomorrow at the same time of day."

"Who is your mistress?" he asked.

"Lady Katherine Golding, the daughter of the Duke of Chatham who has recently moved to Gravesend." She looked up. "Have you heard of her?"

Aiden ran his fingers through the dog's matted fur. Lady Katherine Golding was the woman his stepbrothers were so eager to meet. The heiress of Silverbard. "Yes. I have heard of her arrival."

"Have you heard any gossip concerning her?" Miss Kate's voice came out nonchalant, but Aiden sensed true curiosity behind it.

"I have heard that she is an heiress of great wealth and property. I know of at least two men that will be in pursuit of her." He gave a quiet laugh. "I express my condolences to your mistress. How difficult it must be to have so many unwanted suitors clamoring for her attention."

Her eyes flashed with surprise as she stared at him. "Would *you* not attempt to win her hand?"

Aiden shrugged. "I have not met her. How could I make such a judgement based solely on her status as an heiress? But I am certain she is a lovely young woman if you will endorse her character."

Miss Kate smiled, warm and genuine. For a moment they both simply stared at the other across the brook, and Aiden had to shake himself to regain his thoughts. "Why do you ask? Surely she would not consider a servant."

Her eyes fell along with her smile. "Of course not. Such a match would be extremely improper."

"Extremely." He smiled, shifting the squirming dog in his arms. It seemed Freddy was eager to return to Miss Kate's side, yet Aiden knew that the moment he returned the dog he would no longer have an excuse to remain where he stood. And he wasn't ready to part from Miss Kate just yet.

But something in her disposition had changed, her smiling lips now pinched together in a frown, a crease marking her forehead. "I'm afraid I must be going." She eyed her dog, taking a step toward the fallen tree that crossed the brook.

*Did the woman plan to cross the brook again?* Aiden watched with amusement as she placed one tentative foot on the log.

He stepped forward, grinning without reserve. "Do not move another inch, Miss Kate. I will bring Freddy to you."

Her shoulders slumped in relief, and she offered a soft smile. Aiden stepped onto the log and began walking carefully across it. His two steps of progress were quickly erased as he lost his balance on a knot of wood, falling backward into the water. He hit the

40

muddy bed with a thud and a splash. He managed to hold Freddy above the surface as his own head submerged. He sat up, the dog's hind legs kicking as if preparing to swim.

Another round of musical laughter broke through the water that clogged Aiden's ears. Miss Kate stood with her hands framing her face, pure amusement in her eyes. Aiden sloshed out of the brook, bursting into laughter of his own. "That was entirely Freddy's fault," he said, blinking water from his eyes, watching the ground carefully for any hazards that might cause another fall. "He demanded that I allow him another swim."

Stepping onto dry ground, he looked up, meeting Miss Kate's gaze. Her smile had returned, and what a lovely smile it was. He studied the creases at the corners of her eyes, the dark sweep of her lashes, and the water that still clung to them. His breath hitched as she stared up at him, and it took him a moment to realize that she was reaching for her dog.

He exhaled quickly, the sound mingled with a laugh. "Here is the little scoundrel." He extended Freddy, placing him in her arms. She held the dog tightly against her, rocking him back and forth as one might soothe a child.

She lifted her gaze to Aiden's, the shyness returning to her expression. "I thank you, sir."

He nodded, not bothering to hide his admiration as he watched her. "It was no problem at all. I would

41

gladly sacrifice warm, dry clothing for the sake of an arrogant little scoundrel at any moment."

She fixed him with a teasing glare. "Freddy is not arrogant. He is simply very protective."

Aiden smiled. "And what a worthy person he has chosen to protect."

Her gaze fell as her cheeks grew pink once again. "You are too kind, sir. You do not know me at all."

"That is a problem that I would like to remedy." He brought himself closer to her, reaching out to scratch Freddy's head. "I hope to see you again." He waited, his heart thumping against his chest. "And Freddy as well," he stammered. "I expect Freddy and I are on our way to a steadfast friendship."

She blinked, a look of worry pervading her expression. It quickly faded, replaced by a spark of hope. Her fingers fiddled with the wet fur on Freddy's back. "You might bring Wrinkles and Puff to meet Freddy? I'm certain he would like another friend or two."

Aiden couldn't stop his smile from growing. She wished to see him again too. "Very well." He moved his fingers under the dog's muzzle, scratching his chin. "I will be here, with my two dogs, tomorrow at eleven. If you can join us, we would be most honored."

She drew a deep breath, a smile touching her lips. "And we shall both try not to fall into the brook again."

He laughed. "We shall try."

A shot of pain dug into his hand. He looked down

to see Freddy clamping his jaw down on his thumb. Aiden drew his hand back fast.

Miss Kate gasped. "Freddy! How dare you bite your rescuer? How very naughty of you." She tapped his nose in reprimand. She looked up at Aiden apologetically, but he laughed.

"It seems we have more warming up to do."

She laughed, her lips twisting in a grin. "He does not take well to strangers. But he did seem to like you."

Aiden chuckled. "He likes the taste of me, at least."

Miss Kate fell into a bout of uncontrollable laughter, touching a hand to her waist as she gathered her bearings. Aiden felt he could listen to the sound the entire day, and never grow tired of it.

"I am very sorry," she said as her laughter subsided. "You must think me a complete madwoman. First I fell in a brook and then I laughed in such a fashion." She shook her head, bringing her palm to her forehead.

He studied her rueful expression, a smile still marking his own. "Do not be sorry."

Her gaze darted to his before looking down at her dog. Shy again. "I should be on my way. The mistress will wonder what has kept me for so long."

"You might tell her that you fell in a brook and nearly drowned. She would likely excuse you then."

"Yes, but then she would question the wisdom of ever allowing me to walk Freddy." She bit her lower lip. "I suppose I should... allow Freddy's fur to dry before returning." She took a fistful of his soaking fur, her eyes flicking upward. "The sun is warm today. It should not take long." She searched the clearing for a ray of sunlight, moving to stand beneath it. The dog turned his nose up to the sky, his eyes closing as he enjoyed the warmth. Miss Kate did the same. With her face shrouded in light, she looked positively angelic.

Aiden couldn't stop his feet from following her, moving to a place nearby with a similar amount of sunlight filtering through the trees. He sat down on a large rock, running his fingers through his short dark hair. He caught Miss Kate watching him, her expression curious and intent. She averted her gaze quickly, clutching her dog closer to her.

Aiden hadn't paused to think of the consequences until now, if they were seen together in the middle of the woods. He was not truly a servant, even if he was treated as one. He was the son of a gentleman and the stepson of a marquess. If he was found alone with Miss Kate by anyone of consequence, things would not bode well for her. She could find herself trapped in a marriage with him. He questioned the wisdom of meeting her here again, but not by coincidence. Would it be too dangerous?

He eyed her from across the way, his heart skipping in his chest as she placed a kiss atop the dog's head, smiling down at him lovingly. There was something about her that drew him, a certain genuine joy and wonder at the world. Her independence and resilience were admirable as well. And her willingness to laugh so heartily in the presence of a man she hardly knew... it was extraordinary. He hadn't shared such laughter with another person in years as he just had with Miss Kate. He found it refreshing, and somewhat unsettling, for she reminded him of happier days that he had placed far behind him.

Her expression grew contemplative as she regarded Aiden. "In what household are you employed?"

He hesitated. Did he wish to continue the ruse? He had little choice. "Colborne Hall, the new residence of the Marquess of Aveley."

She drew a quick breath, her expression forced. "They—they have recently arrived in Gravesend, haven't they?"

He nodded. "Yes. Just one week has passed since we arrived." He refrained from extending a warning to her that she might relay to her mistress, that Miles and Evan had their sights set on the heiress.

She pressed her lips together. "This may seem to be a strange question, and I will not pressure you to answer it... but do you have an opinion of the sons, Lord Orsett and Lord Evan Browning? My lady, she—well, she will soon become acquainted with them."

Aiden exhaled through his nostrils, struggling to formulate a response. He searched his mind for one word, one blasted word he could say that would be both honest and positive about his stepbrothers, but he could find nothing. He rubbed his forehead, regarding her solemnly. "I'm afraid I do not know them well enough to make a proper estimation for you, Miss Kate. I keep to my work and prefer not to interfere with the family."

She nodded with understanding, disappointment in her eyes again.

"You seem to care a great deal for the happiness of Lady Katherine," Aiden said, hoping to lighten the weight in her eyes. "She is very fortunate to have you."

She still appeared troubled, even more so when he smiled at her.

She retreated back several steps, leaving the ray of sun and entering the shade of a tree. "Perhaps we might dry quicker by the fire," she said to Freddy. She glanced at Aiden one more time before giving a quick nod. "Good day, sir. Thank you again for rescuing my—my mistress's dog." Her tone had taken on a more serious note, her cheeks flushing.

Aiden stood. "I am honored to have helped."

She gave the faintest smile. "Good day, Mr. Notley."

He wished she would stay a little longer. He didn't care that he would have a lecture awaiting him when he returned to Colborne Hall. He didn't care that their time alone together put both of them at risk of discovery. "Good day, Miss Kate."

At the mere mention of her name, her cheeks colored with a blush. Her eyes filled with curiosity as she turned away from him, tucking Freddy under her arm as she walked back into the thicket. He wished he could walk her home, to ensure she arrived safely.

When she was out of sight, he dropped himself back onto his seat, his legs feeling weaker than usual. His pulse thrummed with energy and strength, brought to life by his new acquaintance. *Kate.* He smiled at the thought of her determination to rescue the dog. Though she treasured the gown her mistress had given her, she didn't value it more than a life, even a life as small as Freddy's. She was a rare sort of woman. He hoped he would have the privilege of discovering more about her.

Standing, he brushed off the back of his breeches before setting off toward Colborne Hall. Rather than emptiness occupying his thoughts while he worked, he now had a much lovelier alternative.

# Chapter 4

Kate stumbled over her wet skirts as she walked through the back door of her new residence, ruining her planned quiet entrance. She crashed against a nearby decorative table, knocking a dusty vase to the ground. It shattered, echoing through the wide and empty hall. She clutched Freddy to her chest as she tiptoed across the marble floors of Timberwell toward her bedchamber.

Her cheeks still felt warm as she walked carefully up the staircase to her room, gripping the bell pull to summon her maid.

Her real maid.

She sat down on her bed, resting her chin on her hands. Why had she thought it wise to pretend to be a lady's maid? She squeezed her eyes shut as regret poured through her stomach. Even so, a smile sneaked its way onto her lips, filling her with a giddy elation

48

that froze her breath in her lungs. *Mr. Aiden Notley.*

Her smile was quickly banished from her face, however, when she remembered a very important detail. He was a servant. If there were ever a match her parents would disapprove of, it was that. *Do not even entertain the thought*, she scolded herself. But how could she not? In the brief time she spent with Mr. Notley in the woods she had felt a connection to him. A desire to come to know his character more. She could not remember the last time she had met a man that seemed so genuine. So kind and honorable. Did that not matter more than a title or fortune?

Oh, why had she pretended to be a maid? She had lied to him. There were times she wished she did not have her dowry and her inheritance—times she wished that she were as ordinary as a maid. Then she could choose to marry a man that was as good and kind as Mr. Notley, and not be forced to give attention to men that only sought her holdings.

She thought of his dark, mussed hair, his sun-darkened skin, and his deep brown eyes. She had never seen a smile like his—the sincerity of it, the lack of reservation. She fell back on her pillows, not caring that the wetness of her hair would soak into them. Why must he be a servant? Setting Freddy down beside her, she watched as he curled into a little wet ball, nestling his head on her stomach.

"Did you find him as charming as I did?" she asked Freddy, turning him over to scratch his belly. "No, of course not. You attempted to bite off his finger." She laughed, the sound turning into a sigh. The fact that Mr. Notley had found Freddy endearing only made *him* more endearing. Good heavens. What was she thinking? A servant!

She could not go to the woods to meet him tomorrow. The mere suggestion had been ridiculous. How improper it would be. Simply because her family moved to Gravesend did not mean she could take on a new identity.

She rolled to her side with a groan. Her door creaked open, the sound quickly followed by a sharp gasp.

"Me lady, what 'as 'appened to you?" Peggy, her maid, rushed to her side. Her eyes rounded like saucers when she saw Kate's torn and dirty gown, and wet, matted hair.

Kate hadn't dared look in the mirror. She sat up, brushing bits of drying twigs from her lap. "I attempted to rescue Freddy from the brook in the woods, and fell in the water." She hesitated to finish. "A man that was passing through rescued him for me."

Peggy's eyebrows raised. She always loved a bit of gossip. Kate didn't dare tell her any further details.

"A man?"

"Yes, a servant. He was quite helpful." Kate stood up, happy to see that her skirts were no longer dripping onto the ground. "If you would be so kind as to assist me in cleaning up for dinner, I would be most grateful."

50

Peggy gave a curtsy, guiding Kate by the arm to her chair in front of the looking glass. Kate cringed at the mud that smeared all over her cheeks and jaw, and the hair that hung drab and heavy over her face. "Oh, dear."

Peggy smiled, searching Kate's curls for buried pins. "I hope you didn't tell this servant of your identity. He'll be spreadin' all kinds of gossip 'bout you fallin' in the water."

She shook her head, disrupting Peggy's search for pins. "I did not tell him. Even if I had, I am certain he would not do such a thing."

Peggy met her eyes in the mirror, a look of curiosity burning there. She remained silent, pulling a comb through Kate's tangled hair. "You best not be tellin' the master about your walk today. He might not let you go again."

Although it wasn't her place to give advice, Kate enjoyed hearing her maid's opinion on matters. She always had a strong one.

"I will not tell him." Kate looked at her reflection, at the smile that still tugged at her lips. How could she ever tell her father that she had found a servant of Lord Aveley's to be intriguing and charming? She could never. It would remain her secret. Hers and Freddy's.

When Peggy finished styling her hair, Kate stood and changed into a clean white dress, smoothing her hands over the soft muslin. She cringed as the tiny cuts on her palms rubbed against the threads. She touched the tiny abrasions, not even upset by them. She never wanted to forget today, as embarrassing as it was to fall into the brook and climb her way out in front of a man. Yet he had not belittled her or censured her. She was certain he had enjoyed her company too.

Peggy went outside the bedchamber, returning with a card in her hand. "From the master." She extended Kate's father's card, where a quick message was scrawled. *Please come to my study at once.*

She took the card from Peggy's outstretched hand and tucked it into her shoe before walking out the door. What could her father want with her? Had he somehow discovered her excursion today? She hoped all remnants of mud and scrapes had been hidden. She would have to make certain not to show her father her scratched palms.

When she reached the ground level, she turned in the direction of the study. She was still memorizing the interior of Timberwell, and it was more difficult than she thought it would be. It was smaller than Silverbard, but still very expansive. She had found several intriguing rooms on the upper levels, the sort of rooms she had always imagined would contain secret passages.

She knocked lightly on the door of the study before her father's voice came through. "Enter."

Kate took a slow step beyond the threshold, meeting her father's eyes with a smile.

"Ah, Kate, come sit." He motioned at the chair

across from him, his eyes twinkling. She swept her skirts beneath her as she sat, tucking her hands in her lap to hide them. She had also forgotten to clean the mud from her fingernails.

"Good afternoon, Papa. How may I be of assistance?" She looked across to him expectantly.

He straightened a stack of papers in front of him. Kate's stomach turned as it always did when she saw his abundance of papers. If she was truly to own an estate like Silverbard one day, she would have much to learn about managing it. She hoped her father's health would hold for many more years, for more reasons than one.

"I have called you here to discuss a few of your upcoming social invitations here in Gravesend," he said.

Kate's face fell. Oh, how she despised sociality among men that knew of her fortune. She had forgotten her plight since meeting Mr. Notley in the woods. "Social invitations?"

"Yes, there have been several."

*Of course there have been.* Kate's posture stiffened as she listened to her father warily.

"First, as I indicated before, Lord Aveley and his sons, Lord Orsett and Lord Evan Browning would like to receive us in three weeks in their new residence of Colborne Hall. They have informed me that their servants are hard at work preparing the estate for guests, so it will be some time before they will receive us, but they assured me they are quite eager to make your acquaintance." He smiled. "I would advise you most strongly to consider Lord Orsett above all other suitors at this time. He will be a marquess, and from what I have heard, he is a very agreeable young man."

At the mention of *Colborne Hall* and *servants,* all Kate could think of was Mr. Notley, busy dusting and pruning and scraping grime from the floors. Perhaps Lord Orsett was just as pleasant as Mr. Notley, she tried to assure herself. But she could not bring herself to believe it.

Her father raised one thick eyebrow, creasing his forehead with three deep wrinkles. "Well? Are you looking forward to it?"

"Yes," she stammered, her voice coming off dull. "Very much."

He let out a long sigh, apparently sensing her discontent. "My dear. I seek to match you with Lord Orsett because I desire a respectable position for you in society. I desire your happiness and comfort through all of your life. If you marry Lord Orsett, with his inheritance of Colborne Hall and your inheritance of Silverbard, you will own the most land in the county. Do you realize the significance of this?"

She gave a slow nod, her stomach sinking still. "But Papa... perchance I do not like Lord Orsett at all?"

He chewed his bottom lip, his brows drawing together. He never did appreciate when she looked at him the way she currently was, with her eyes wide with concern and her lips pouting. "Oh, Kate." He drew a deep breath. "Will you assure me that you will at least *try* to like him? Marriages are, at their core—much to the universal dismay of young women—a business agreement."

"Yes, I know." She sighed. "I will try to like him." All foolish hope she had entertained of becoming further acquainted with Mr. Notley was quickly fleeing, fading into the books that rested on the shelves of her father's study. How could she simply leave him with his dogs in the woods tomorrow, waiting for her? Perhaps she could see him one more time before avoiding him forever. After all, she was not seeing him as Lady Katherine, she was seeing him as Miss Kate. There was a great difference between the two. Lady Katherine was refined and wealthy and resigned to court who her father chose, and Miss Kate was happy, somewhat unrefined, and free to court who she chose. Even a servant.

Her father stared at her with his stern brow for several seconds before giving a nod. "Very well. There is another matter I wish to discuss with you. Since we are new to this area, I would like to introduce our family to the town by way of a ball. Timberwell has a very spacious ballroom. We would like to host this ball on your behalf, as a way to introduce you to the people of Gravesend and the surrounding towns. We want to ensure it is known that you are out in society and entirely marriageable. I have searched extensively to find all the men of this area that are eligible and that I would approve of marrying you."

He plucked a sheet of foolscap out from the pile in front of him, sliding it across the desk so Kate could read it. "This is a list of all the men I find worthy by way of holdings and property to make a match with you. They and their families will all receive invitations to the ball. I intend to hold this ball in two weeks. It will allow you to make Lord Orsett's acquaintance prior to accepting their dinner invitation."

Kate's dread only intensified. How could she choose a husband out of a short list of approximately ten gentlemen? There were thousands in England, and she could only make her selection from ten? She calmed her anxiety. At least she would not be forced to only consider Lord Orsett.

"Well? Did you hear me?" Kate's father's voice cut through her thoughts, light and filled with amusement. How could he find her distress amusing?

"Yes. I was simply thinking of what I might wear."

He chuckled, drawing the parchment back to his pile, a satisfied smile on his lips. "Not to worry. I will have the most beautiful gown you have ever worn ordered, as well as a new pair of dancing slippers. You must stand apart from all the other young ladies there. The town must know of our standing and your wealth. You will look lovely." He set his spectacles atop his nose, staring down at another piece from his stack. "I have allocated significant funds for this ball. Your

56

mother will work with you to determine the clothing and hairstyle. I plan to invite a great number of
people, and we must ensure they all remember you. I
daresay you will have dozens of calls and bouquets the
next day."

Kate couldn't comprehend how discussing and
planning this ball brought such joy to her father. It
only made her feel ill. She didn't want to be the center of attention at an extravagant ball. She wanted to
laugh until she couldn't breathe, not wear a corset so
tight that it did the same, or stifle her laughter and
keep her smiles polite and minimal.

"Kate. You seem quite distracted today. Is there
something you wish to tell me?" Her father's eyes had
lifted from his papers, staring down the bridge of his
nose at her.

"No, not at all, I—" she stopped, an idea striking
her. She sighed. "I am just distraught about the towns-
people I saw on my walk today with Freddy. There is
more poverty in Gravesend than I have seen in Sheffield. It breaks my heart."

Her father gave her a compassionate smile. "I am
glad to hear you are so sensitive to such matters. An
amiable quality, to be sure."

She hesitated over her next words. "You did say
the ballroom of Timberwell is quite large. I have seen
it myself, and I believe we could host a substantial
amount of guests."

"We can indeed."

She swallowed, wringing her hands together beneath the table. "Do you remember during the last Christmastide when we invited the less fortunate to a dinner and dance?"

His expression shifted, apprehension filling it. "I do."

"Do you suppose…that we may invite the less fortunate to attend our ball as well? Our guests might extend our invitations to their servants."

Her father stared at her, his eyes rounding. She waited, her heart thudding. After a prolonged moment, her father burst into boisterous laughter, slapping his hand down on his desk. "You cannot be serious, my dear."

Heat leapt to her cheeks. She had known her request was ridiculous. "They will add a much needed frivolity to the ball." Her voice was weak.

He shook his head, chuckling under his breath. "I will not transform a ball in your honor to a charity. We will save such an event for the Christmastide."

Kate set her jaw against further words, but could not help speaking again. "Do you mean to say that kindness is a quality to only be exercised at a designated time of year? Kindness should not have beginning nor end within us. It should be an inborn part of our character at all hours, days, and months."

Her father's frown deepened. "Do you realize the censure that would fall upon our family if we had servants as guests at our ball? It simply cannot happen. I am sorry, Kate, but you must learn to tame your absurd notions. I hope you will not host such balls at Silverbard when I am gone." He fixed her with a stern look, one she rarely saw on his face.

She averted her eyes. "Of course not, Papa."

He sighed again, the sound he always made when he witnessed his daughter's dejection. "My dear. Do not be upset with me. I could not bear it." He reached forward with his hand, intending to hold hers. She looked up, keeping her hands clasped together beneath the table.

The large clock on the wall behind her father chimed, the sound cutting through the awkward silence of the room. Kate counted three loud and deep chimes. Her mother hated that clock, but Kate felt fortunate to have it stop her father from further questioning.

"I do not feel well," she said. "Please excuse me."

Her father sat back in his chair with a nod, frustration looming in his eyes. Kate did not blame him for rejecting her request. She had been absurd, as he said, to have even asked. Her father wanted the best life for her, and she was grateful for that. He had given her so much, it was time she gave him something in return. If he desired for her to marry a man from that list, then she would do it. She had a duty to uphold. Her heart could not interfere. She could not go see Mr. Notley the next day. To do so would be detrimental to her resolve to obey her father.

When she stood in the hallway, she breathed the

fresh and open air, trying to calm the dread that pooled in her chest. She would never see Mr. Notley again, but that did not mean she couldn't treasure the memory. And she would treasure it always.

# Chapter 5

Aiden brought his needle through the thick leather of a pair of riding boots, his fingers shaking with the precision it required. When he competed the stitch, he held it up for Mr. Haskett to critique.

As he had many times that day, the man appeared rather astonished. "Perfect. I can find no fault in it." He looked up from the boot, meeting Aiden's eyes with renewed surprise. "You must have done this before."

Aiden shook his head, returning his needle to the leather once again. "I have not. My mother purchased many shoes when I was a child, and loved to show me every detail. I often wondered how they were made. She had one pair of slippers that were her favorite, and I have never seen such pristine workmanship and skill. She was very proud of them." He smiled, the memory overtaking his thoughts and filling him with distant joy.

Mr. Haskett picked up his own project, a pair of ladies half boots. "Astonishing. I am quite impressed. Are you in possession of those slippers?"

Aiden nodded.

"Would you consider bringing them to the shop so I may study them? I am very curious."

"Yes, of course. I'm certain you will find them as enchanting as my mother did."

Mr. Haskett sat back with a satisfied smile. "We do have an order from the Duchess of Chatham to construct a new pair of dancing slippers for her daughter. She requested that they be silk with many embellishments. She requested lace, ribbon rosettes, and intricate beadwork. We will need to begin straight away if we hope to finish by the Timberwell ball in a fortnight. They are sending invitations to the neighbors immediately, and we will be receiving many orders."

At the mention of the duchess's daughter, Aiden's thoughts traveled once again to the young lady, Miss Kate, in the woods. He hoped he would have an opportunity to slip away from Mr. Haskett for long enough to meet her as they had planned. He glanced at the nearby clock, seeing that the time read half past ten.

"If you would like, I can fetch the slippers now," Aiden said. "My residence is not far."

Mr. Haskett glanced up, his suppressed eagerness now coming into light. "Yes. That would be most opportune. I suspect there is much I may learn from these slippers if you learned so much with just a simple glance at them."

Aiden set the riding boots aside, his own excitement mounting. He would have just enough time to reach Colborne Hall, fetch his dogs and the slippers, and meet Miss Kate in the woods for a time before returning to the cordwainer. "Very well. I will fetch them now." Aiden smiled, turning swiftly for the door.

"You may choose to take a midday meal as well. Be back no later than twelve." Mr. Haskett motioned at the clock.

"Yes, sir."

Aiden ran the short distance to Colborne Hall, hoping to afford himself as much time as possible to spend with Miss Kate. Careful to avoid his stepfather and stepbrothers, he sneaked to his bedchamber to retrieve his mother's slippers. They lay in a box with his father's pocket watch. He removed the slippers and the watch, cradling them gently in his hands as he slid them into the bag that crossed his body. Outside, he untethered his dogs, leashing them both before setting off for the woods.

As he walked, he withdrew the watch, checking the time. It was precisely eleven. He walked faster, his dogs trotting along beside him. When the brook came into view, he found a large rock to sit on, tying his dogs to a nearby branch. He would unleash them once he knew they would behave kindly toward Miss Kate and Freddy.

He watched the trees where she had departed the last time. What would she think of Wrinkles and Puff? Under normal circumstances he would have been embarrassed to admit that he had once named his dogs such ridiculous names, but nothing about his interaction with Miss Kate had been normal. He had never felt so at ease conversing with a pretty young woman before, and certainly not one who he met in such an unconventional way.

As the minutes wore on, she still did not appear between the trees. He checked the pocket watch. Fifteen minutes had passed. The woods were silent, just a soft rustling of the leaves and the trickle of the brook beside him. His dogs stood under the shade of a tree, both straining against their leashes, seeking the warmth of a ray of sunshine that touched the nearby ground.

Just when Aiden was bound to give up and return to the cordwainer, he heard frantic and light footfalls in the distance, followed by heavier ones and rapid breathing.

"Freddy!" A harsh whisper reached him. He stood up, a grin already finding its way to his face. Why did she feel the need to whisper? He waited for Freddy to come skittering through the trees, determined to catch the dog before it could find itself in the water. As predicted, the little gray dog came running straight toward Aiden, changing his course when he saw Wrinkles and Puff beneath the tree. Aiden's two dogs stiffened, barking in friendly tones as Freddy approached.

64

Aiden turned his gaze back to the trees. The heavier footfalls had stopped, but he could still hear a quiet breathing, short and jagged, as if intentionally softened.

"Miss Kate?" Aiden called. Several seconds passed before she finally emerged between the trees, her eyes cast down in embarrassment and apparent regret. She wore a different dress than the day before, one still far too nice for a lady's maid. He studied her intricate curls and smooth skin. *A maid?* A breathtaking one.

"Good morning, Mr. Notley," she said, her eyes flicking to his quickly before darting away. Her hair had flown back from her face from her chase after Freddy, leaving her cheeks pink with exertion. Her chest and shoulders rose and fell with her heavy breathing. She no longer tried to conceal the sound. "Freddy chewed through his leash in the night and I did not know of it. I intended to take him for a turn around the Timberwell property, but the leash snapped the moment he pulled on it. He ran straight for the woods. I suppose he was determined to find you." She spoke with a scowl, placing her hand against her waist.

Aiden smiled as Freddy approached him. He scooped the dog up, noticing the severed rope that hung from his neck. "You are a scoundrel after all," Aiden said in a censuring voice. "How dare you escape Miss Kate and make her run all this way? Your impish behavior yesterday was quite enough." Freddy stretched his neck to sniff Aiden's face.

Miss Kate suppressed a smile, concern pinching her brow. "I should not have come. I am very sorry."

Aiden tipped his head in confusion. "You did not intend to come?"

She met his eyes. "I began to doubt the wisdom of it, sir."

He studied her stoic expression and the intense regret in her features. He found his study of her face so enjoyable, he did not realize how long he had been staring at her. He shook himself, turning his attention back to the dog he held as he walked closer to her. "What is there to doubt? I'm certain your mistress will be pleased that Freddy has so much reason to be happy today. He has made two new friends and has been reunited with another." He gave her a winning smile, hoping to see one on her own face.

Her eyes glinted with amusement and her lips twitched. "I suppose it is acceptable for a man and woman to meet alone if it concerns a matter of business. And my mistress views her dog's happiness as a very serious matter of business indeed."

He nodded. "Very true."

She stared up at him, a true smile pulling at her cheeks.

"You are doing your mistress and Freddy a kindness by being here," he said. "Kindness is never to be delayed or suppressed."

Her eyes flashed with admiration, enough to make his heart stall in his chest. "It seems that very few people share that sentiment."

"But not you." Aiden's gaze remained steadfast on hers. "You hold it to great importance."

She looked down. "How could I not? So many people have been kind to me throughout my life. I must pay my debts somehow."

Her humility and grace struck him. "We are all debtors of some sort." He thought of his residence with Lord Aveley and how it was contingent on his upkeep of the estate. Would he ever free himself of his stepfather's influence? Thinking of the months, even years that could lay ahead of him before he could gather sufficient funds to rent his own home, his hope grew faint.

A deep bark came from Wrinkles, the Pug's face contorting eagerly as he stared across the way at Miss Kate, straining against his leash. Aiden chuckled, moving to remove the restraint and replacing it at Freddy's neck instead.

The Pug ran to Miss Kate's side, stopping hesitantly a few paces away. She smiled down at him, bending to pat his head. He set to licking her hand, and her laugh, light and pleasant, rang through the air. Her eyes lifted as she stroked the dog's head. "Mr. Notley, you have named him well. He does have many endearing wrinkles."

Her guard seemed to have dropped, at least for the moment. Aiden knew his visit would have to be short. The cordwainer was likely growing anxious for his return. "You may thank a moment of ridiculousness on my part for such a name."

She continued laughing before straightening her posture and moving to greet the Pomeranian who had begun spinning around Freddy in a quick circle, their leashes tangling.

"You must be Puff." She untangled the leashes and scooped up the dog from his running, holding him close to her. She glanced at Aiden, pure delight in her green eyes. "He is very sweet."

"You might commission your mistress to allow you to trade Puff for Freddy. I will tame the little scoundrel and you will have a sweet dog to look after rather than an unscrupulous one."

She returned Puff to the ground, shaking her head. "It is Freddy's pluck that endears him to me. He does not fear the results of his actions. He does not fear the judgements of others. He does as he pleases without a second thought. He is free and courageous and determined." Her voice carried a tone Aiden hadn't heard before—a strong, resolved undercurrent. "I should like to be more like him one day."

Aiden was finding more and more to admire about Miss Kate with each minute that passed. *Blast it.* Why had he lied to her? He wished to be more like Freddy too. If he took Miss Kate's sentiments to heart then he could find a way to escape his stepfather's influence. He would have done more to prevent the selling of his childhood home and his parents' possessions. He would not have agreed to Lord Aveley's demands that he pretend to be a servant.

"Do you find my ideas strange?" she asked. "I expect it is not normal to wish to be like a dog." Amusement still shone in her eyes, but curiosity burned behind it.

"Not at all. I think there is much to learn from animals."

She smiled, and he found his thoughts fleeing as he stared into her eyes. Seeking a distraction, Aiden reached in his bag and withdrew his father's pocket watch. If he was late Mr. Haskett would have his head.

"I wish I could stay longer, but I must be going." Aiden heard the regret in his own voice.

"Does your master need you back so soon?"

He nodded. "I'm afraid so."

She turned her attention to the dogs. "I am glad they were able to become acquainted. Freddy will never wish to leave. I don't wish to leave either." Her eyes fluttered up to his hesitantly. Aiden was not a stranger to flirtatious women. He had seen them interact with his stepbrothers as they sought the prize of Lord Orsett's title. But Miss Kate was different. When she glanced up at him in such a shy way, it was not an attempt to be coy. It was genuine and sweet and entirely too endearing. He took a step back with great effort, wishing he could stay and continue learning more about her.

But why was he entertaining thoughts of courting a lady's maid? It could never be. She was occupied with her work and he with his. And if he did allow his feelings to progress and they continued to see one another, he could never support a marriage. So why did he come today? It had been a mistake.

Yet it didn't feel like a mistake, and that made it all the more frustrating.

"Best of luck with your work," she said in a quiet voice.

"And you with yours. Please take one of my leashes to convey Freddy home." He turned away from her, untethering Freddy's restraint from the tree and extending the rope to her.

She took it, her hand brushing over his, light and small. His pulse thudded. His gaze fell to her hands. They were smooth, soft, without the slightest sign of past labor. *A maid?* he repeated in his mind, the disbelief growing firmer. He shunned his doubts. A lady's maid wouldn't have to labor much with her hands, besides arranging hair and dresses.

"Is this another gown your mistress gave you?" he asked, unable to help his curiosity.

Her cheeks darkened as she stared down at the flowing fabric of her skirts. "Yes." She swallowed. "She—she orders new gowns often and rather than dispose of them, she gives them to me."

"She must be very kind." He wished he had the privilege of working among such a kind family.

Miss Kate's blush intensified as she wrapped the leash around her hand, pulling Freddy along as he resisted, trying to return to the other dogs. She seemed to be in a sudden hurry.

70

"When may I see you again?" Aiden asked, his voice too quick.

She stopped, her brows contracting, forming a crease between them. She hesitated for a long moment, as if torn over a certain decision. Why did she seem so troubled by his company? Did she share his fears of growing too close?

"I will be quite busy for what remains of this week."

"And next week?" Aiden asked.

She began pulling the dog toward the trees, that same troubling expression still permeating her face.

"Think of the poor dogs." Aiden nodded first toward Freddy and then toward Wrinkles and Puff. "How unkind it would be for us to introduce them only to force them to never see one another again."

Her lips pinched, the corners drifting upward. "That would be very unkind."

He nodded firmly, his smile unreserved. Her hesitation returned, and she gave a swift smile before turning on her heel and hurrying into the trees.

"You didn't give me an answer," he said, chuckling.

She hurried on her way, as if she hadn't heard him.

He snapped his watch closed and dropped it in his bag, walking with large strides in the direction of the cordwainer's shop. Mr. Haskett expected his return by twelve, so he had a scant fifteen minutes to return his dogs to Colborne Hall and get back to the shop.

And one was without a leash.

Fortunately the jaunt home and back to the shop totaled less than a mile and a half, and he managed to arrive just as the hands of the cordwainer's clock struck twelve. Mr. Haskett glanced up from his work, his observant eyes likely noting the sweat on Aiden's brow.

"My apologies, sir." Aiden sat down, opening his bag to reveal his mother's dancing slippers. The stern focus of Mr. Haskett's eyes immediately softened as they took in the beautiful shoes.

He reached out with delicate touch, running his fingers over the sole. "How exquisite."

Aiden nodded, taking a moment to admire them himself. Even after a few short hours of learning the art of a cordwainer, his appreciation of the workmanship had increased tenfold. The soles, soft and flexible, were sewn with tiny, seemingly indestructible stitches, not a single line out of place. The silken fabric that enveloped it was made of a pale, shimmering gold, a color difficult to achieve with dye. The pointed toe was decorated with a trio of fabric rosettes, all pale blue, with pearls and tiny silver beads among them.

"Extraordinary," Mr. Haskett said as he continued to examine the seams and stitches. "Where were these shoes constructed?"

"I believe it was in London." Aiden recalled an image of his mother, spinning across the ballroom of Thornwall with his father, laughing as her feet, dressed in those very shoes, glided effortlessly over the polished floors.

"We will create nothing short of this beauty for Lady Katherine Golding." Mr. Haskett grinned with rapture. "And you will be the prime constructor of her slippers."

"Me?" Aiden couldn't believe Mr. Haskett would entrust such an important project to him.

"You possess a natural talent, and your stitches on those boots are nearly as perfect as these." He touched a finger to the sole of the slipper. "We must secure the Duke and Duchess as returning customers. The neighboring towns are not far, and both have means to construct fine shoes. We must win Lady Katherine's loyalty."

Although Aiden doubted his ability, Mr. Haskett seemed certain of it. Aiden gave a slow nod. "I will try my best."

"I am glad to hear that. The moment we receive word of the selected color, we may begin. I do hope they inform us soon. Such a project will take days, especially for an apprentice." Mr. Haskett winked, resuming his study of the slippers.

Aiden smiled, picking up his work where he left it. If he possessed a talent like Mr. Haskett believed, then perhaps with a bit of work he could escape Lord Aveley sooner than he thought. Determination surged in his chest as he punctured the leather with his needle.

# Chapter 6

"What do you think of this one?" Kate's mother sat beside her on the sofa, a series of fashion plates on her lap. The ball at Timberwell was the talk of all of Gravesend, and every man within ten miles was set on attending, if only to meet Kate and have an attempt to win her hand.

She could not wait until it was over.

Three days had passed since her father had told her of his intention to hold a ball. It would be held in less than a fortnight, and it was long past time for Kate to select the colors and embellishments of her gown. The town modiste was buried in work with all the other ladies that would be attending the ball. Kate's mother did not seem to be worried though, for she knew Kate's gown would become the modiste's top priority upon its order. The same would be for the new dancing slippers they would be ordering. All that was left to decide was the color, and Kate's mother had much to say on the subject.

"If your gown is indeed a robin's egg blue, then you should have a neutral or contrasting shoe. You are a lovely dancer, so I should like to draw attention to your feet. The skirts will have a train following behind, of course, but the front will be raised enough to show your feet and to allow you necessary freedom while dancing." Her mother pointed at a drawing of rosettes on a pair of dancing slippers. "I would suggest an embellishment such as this. As for the color, a golden silk would be just the thing. Or perhaps a rose pink."

Kate envisioned the colors and nodded. "That sounds perfect." Her voice came out dull. It didn't escape her mother's notice. Her eyebrows lowered, her elation dropping.

"You mustn't act as if this ball is a burden. We are hosting it just for you, to introduce you to this new area of England. There are many fine suitors here and we hope for you to make your best impression upon them. You will not impress anyone if you sulk about with that scowl."

Kate's anger mounted suddenly, clutching in her chest. "They will be impressed no matter how I behave. They are already impressed with me and they have neither met me nor seen my face. They are impressed with the rumor of my inheritance, and that is all. I could be old and unsightly and dressed in rags, but so long as I have thirty thousand pounds and a beautiful estate, I will be wanted." She took a heavy breath, emotion choking her.

Her mother's own scowl tightened. "Katherine!" she gasped, her voice soft and chilling. "You act as if—as if you would rather be a pauper than an heiress. Do you understand how very fortunate you are to have so much? Here we are ordering an intricate gown and slippers for you, and you act as if you would *prefer* to wear rags."

Kate blinked, her anger fading as quickly as it came. "Yes. I am sorry. I should not have raised my voice to you, Mama. Please forgive me."

Her mother was right. Kate was so very blessed and fortunate in material possessions. There were many who were not. Yet she felt cursed in other areas of her life. How—how could she choose one of the men from her father's list? How could she choose one of them when all she could think of was Mr. Aiden Notley?

She hadn't meant to venture to the woods the day before. She had been determined to avoid him, to guard her heart against believing and hoping for things that could never be. But she had been weak. She had ventured outside with Freddy, hoping only to catch a glimpse of Aiden as he entered the woods, or came out on the path near her home. But then Freddy had broken through his leash and she had chased him, losing her choice in the matter.

She had never met a man like Aiden, and she doubted she ever would. He was humble and kind and shared many of her opinions. He loved her dog, as scoundrelly as he could be at times. If he knew she was the Duke's daughter, he would likely act differently toward her. He would understand the glaring space between their social stations. He was noble enough, good enough, that she was certain he would let her go once he was made aware of it.

But she didn't want him to let her go.

Why could he not be Lord Orsett? Why did he have to be the servant of the man she was being encouraged to marry? It was unfair.

Kate realized her mother had been watching her, a deep curiosity in her eyes. Turning her attention back to the fashion plates, Kate tried to appear nonchalant. "For the gown, may we add embroidered gold threads in the skirts to match the slippers? With a deeper blue for the sash?"

Her mother gave a slow nod, her curiosity still evident. "I will add it to the order."

Kate gave a shaky smile, forcing the expression to replace the unrest that surged within her. "Very well. I look forward to wearing it." Kate would never pretend to look forward to the *ball*.

Her mother smiled, the expression just as forced as her daughter's. "Would you like to go to town today to see the fabrics? I have already sent your measurements to the modiste."

Kate hesitated, but decided that a trip to town would be a welcome excursion. If she stayed home with her thoughts all day, she would likely be driven mad. "That sounds wonderful, Mama. I would like that very much."

\* \* \*

They took their curricle to town, the horses lively and quick as they pulled them along on the short drive. Kate closed her eyes, enjoying the light breeze on her skin. She wore her most simple morning dress, in part to irritate her mother, who had wanted her to wear her most extravagant gown in public to draw attention, and in part because it was comfortable and light. She hated the heaviness of layered skirts and embellishments in the summertime.

When they arrived at the modiste, Kate agreed with her mother that the silken, pale blue fabric there would be perfect for her gown. The modiste insisted on taking Kate's measurements herself to ensure their accuracy. A servant had already been sent to deliver their official order for Kate's dancing slippers to the cordwainer, so all that remained was the final decision on the gown.

Madame Boisseau touched Kate's shoulders, turning her to face the opposite wall. She measured the width of her shoulders, then the length of her back, jotting down notes as she went. Kate held perfectly still.

Until she saw Aiden out the front window.

She let out a tiny gasp, stepping down from the modiste's platform as quickly as her legs would allow, hurrying away from the sight of the window. She peered out from her hiding place behind a mannequin, watching the dark sweep of Aiden's hair as he conversed with someone outside the shop. She could imagine the smile in his voice and the joyful sparkle in his brown eyes.

"Lady Katherine, what are you doing over there?" The modiste's voice carried a hint of annoyance. "I am not finished with you." The woman, with her thick, sausage-like curls and rounded cheeks, did not seem the sort of woman to affect a terrifying glare, but here she was, staring down the bridge of her nose at Kate with unarguable demand.

"Kate," Her mother looked up from the shopping list she had been studying. "Return to the platform at once."

Kate eyed the window again, silently praying that Aiden would not venture inside or glance behind him and see her being measured for a gown. If he noticed, her ruse would be over. He would likely despise her for lying to him. She could not bear the thought of him hating her.

With slow steps, she made her way back to the platform, allowing the disgruntled Madame Boisseau to finish her measurements. She worked quickly, as if she feared Kate would scurry away again. Kate breathed deeply, her gaze flicking out the window every five seconds to ensure Aiden had not seen her. When the modiste finally finished, Kate stepped down, moving far away from the window and pretending to examine the fabrics across the shop. She didn't know whether to be relieved or disappointed that she had not had the opportunity to speak to Aiden.

She decided she should be relieved. She could not have him discovering her true identity.

He was likely here in town on an errand from his master. The thought drove disappointment through her, another sharp reminder of her hopelessness toward him.

"Come now, Kate," her mother said, her footsteps approaching behind her. "We have already selected our fabrics for your gown."

Kate didn't dare step outside, not when Aiden stood nearby, but her mother wrapped her fingers around Kate's elbow, pulling her toward the door. Kate reached up and pressed the brim of her bonnet downward, her heart pounding. The moment they stepped outside, she turned her face away from Aiden, pulling against her mother's grip in order to walk faster.

"Good heavens, my dear. What is your hurry?"

"The sun is so very hot." Kate fanned her face, her shoulders relaxing as they achieved a safe distance from Aiden's place on the road.

"You might have brought your parasol if you desire more shade." Her mother's unapologetic tone was interrupted by the voice of a nearby woman.

"Your grace, how do you do?" A woman that appeared to be similar in age to Kate's mother stopped them on their path.

Her mother smiled, a bright and kind expression that had been absent the entire day. "Lady Gilbert. I am quite well. And you?"

"Very well."

Kate glanced over her shoulder, her stomach sinking as she saw Aiden walking with large strides in her direction. He did not appear to have seen her, but he soon would if he continued.

Breaking away from her mother's grasp, she walked to the other side of the street, making her way toward the milliner's shop across the way. She turned her back to Aiden, staring at a straw bonnet in the window. His reflection passed behind her before stopping, his head turning in her direction.

*No. No. No.*

He took two steps closer. "Kate, is that you?" He spoke in a friendly voice, surprise evident within it.

Her stomach grew sick with dread. How could she speak to him as if they were friends with her mother so nearby, watching the exchange? She turned her head slightly, keeping her voice low. "Good morning, Mr. Notley."

"Where is Freddy this morning?" His eyes, deep brown and framed in dark lashes, calmed her nerves, forcing her to relax. Before she knew it, a smile had leapt to her lips.

"He is under severe reprimand. He is not allowed to leave the property until the start of next week."

Aiden chuckled, looking down at the cobblestones. "I thought you planned to reward him for good behavior?"

Kate glanced over her shoulder, catching the eye of her mother. She stiffened. "Yes, but he hasn't any good behavior to reward of late."

Aiden's laugh heightened her senses, and she turned toward him once again. Her mother had seen them speaking. She did not have much time.

"What brings you to town?" he asked. "Are you accompanying Lady Katherine?"

She shook her head. "I was... fetching samples of the fabrics she will be using for her ball gown and slippers."

"I see." Mr. Notley's smile grew, a set of matching creases appearing in both his cheeks. She looked away, the sight causing her heart to skip. Sunlight came through the clouds, bright and intense, bringing golden streaks forward in his eyes. She felt trapped—trapped by his closeness and trapped by her mother. She couldn't make an excuse to leave and flee to her mother's side, and she couldn't remain speaking to him or her mother would question her excessively.

She stared at the bonnet in the window again, feeling Aiden's gaze on the side of her face.

"You look well." His voice came close to her ear, a

shyness entering it that she hadn't heard before. Her cheeks immediately flamed, and she dared a glance at his face. The sincerity, the admiration that glowed there entirely disarmed her. A smile pulled on her lips, and she didn't try to suppress it. The sweetness of his compliment had nothing to do with her fortune, or the extravagance of her gown or slippers. Sudden tears burned behind her eyes, brought to life by Aiden's kindness. Had she effected him irrevocably as he had her? She wished she knew the answers.

"I must be going," she whispered.

He nodded, his shyness persisting as she stepped away, stealing one last glance at his face before turning toward her mother and Lady Gilbert. She walked with her head down, hoping Aiden would walk away before he saw her join them.

As she approached, Lady Gilbert dismissed herself from the duchess's company, apparently sensing the disapproving lecture that was soon to be delivered to Kate. Rather than stop by her mother's side, Kate continued walking toward their curricle.

"Kate!" her mother's hissed whisper trailed behind her, but Kate continued walking, increasing the speed of her footfalls until she had rounded the corner of a new street, safe from Aiden's view.

"Katherine! Stop walking and look at me."

She drew a deep breath, turning to her mother with squared shoulders.

"Please explain what you were doing conversing so

closely with a—with a *servant?*" Her mother spoke the word as if it disgusted her.

Kate did not know how to explain. How could she tell her mother that she had been meeting with that very man in the woods...alone? She couldn't tell her.

"He has expertise in dog training, Mama. He saw me walking with Freddy just the other day, and he offered a few pieces of advice on how to tame him. He was simply inquiring after the success of his advice. There is nothing scandalous about it, not to worry." Kate couldn't keep the sardonic tone from her voice. If she and Aiden were discovered, it would become a scandalous situation indeed. The daughter of a duke fraternizing with a servant of the very man she was expected to marry. Her cheeks flushed at the very thought.

"He was standing... rather close to you." Her mother's anger had reached her eyes. "I would advise you to seek help with your dog elsewhere. Your father may accompany you to the stables to receive training lessons from one of our grooms. Surely they would know how to manage a dog."

Kate nodded, relief flooding through her. She hadn't thought her mother would so readily believe her story. "You are right. That sounds like a much more proper alternative."

Appeased by her daughter's swift agreement, her mother put on a smile, smoothing the creases of anger that had marked her normally docile face. "Good."

"Good." Kate repeated her mother's word, but she did not feel it. There was nothing good about her current situation. The next time she saw Aiden, she would bid him farewell and pray that he never discovered the truth about who she was. She preferred that he not know.

A thought struck her, filling her with dread. If she married Lord Orsett, Aiden would become her servant. He would know everything.

Thankfully her mother didn't try to make conversation on the ride home. She simply clutched her lists in her lap and watched the passing hills and marshes. Kate tried to think of less dreadful thoughts, but it was futile. No matter how many suitors sought her dances at the ball, she would think only of Aiden and how he could never be hers.

And what a dreadful thought that was.

# Chapter 7

Aiden didn't finish the pair of riding boots until midnight, working by candlelight in the center of the cordwainer's shop. Mr. Haskett had fallen asleep at his desk, his head resting on the bend of his elbow. He had finished his latest project several hours before.

As Aiden finished threading the laces, he held the sturdy boots up to the light, a weary smile tugging at his mouth. He had labored over the boots for days, and they were finally finished. The satisfaction that came was invigorating. He could see himself happily working on similar shoes for many years.

Mr. Haskett shifted from his spot at his desk, his spectacles falling askew on his face. He sat up, checking the clock. "How the devil did I sleep for so long?" he said in a hoarse voice.

Aiden chuckled, standing up with a stretch. He

stooped over to pick up the finished boots, turning them toward Mr. Haskett for inspection.

Mr. Haskett straightened his spectacles, taking one boot in his hand, then the other, turning them over to examine all angles. "Extraordinary."

Aiden had heard Mr. Haskett use that word to describe his work many times. "Truly?"

"Indeed." Mr. Haskett set the boots down on a shelf, tying a tag to the laces. "Mr. Clumpet will be quite pleased with them, I believe."

Aiden's elation continued to grow, pride for his work making up for the ache in his back and fingers. He had been making use of the early hours of the morning to clean and prepare Colborne Hall for guests, and he had almost finished. Balancing his responsibilities there with his apprenticeship had been no small task, and as a result he hadn't slept more than three hours each night for nearly a week.

"You have quite a talent, Notley." Mr. Haskett gave him a genuine smile. "I am glad to have taken you on. If you can manage to create a pair of slippers as exquisite as your mother's for Lady Katherine Golding, I will think you capable of miracles."

Aiden laughed, rubbing his eyes to clear the splotches of light that burned behind his eyelids. "I will try my best. You may need to school me a little further in making a lady's shoe. I imagine it is quite different."

"Very different. It requires a gentle touch, a delicate handling. The feet of ladies are much smaller."

"Perhaps Lady Katherine has feet as large as Mr. Clumpet's."

Mr. Haskett chuckled. "I should hope not. She would have to be an ogre at the very least."

"And all the men of Gravesend would still desire her for her fortune." Aiden stared out the dark window of the shop. He thought of his conversation with Miss Kate concerning her mistress. Aiden knew how careless men (and women) could be in their pursuit of wealth. They would toy with a person's heart without any regret in order to obtain it. With the upcoming ball, Aiden knew of at least two men that would be seeking the Duke's daughter for those very purposes.

When he had seen Miss Kate in town today, she had still worn her troubled expression. He wished he knew was was troubling her. He hated to see it.

After bidding Mr. Haskett farewell, Aiden walked back to Colborne hall. The moment he entered the front doors, he heard the sound of Evan's grating laughter coming from the dining room. He glanced in the doorway as he passed. Miles and Evan each sat at the ends of the table, a tall bottle of brandy beside each of them.

"You think you'll win her over?" Miles scoffed. "I'm the future marquess. You will always have nothing but a courtesy title."

"But I am more charming," Evan said, the words slurred. "And more handsome."

"Who told you that? Your reflection?"

Evan gave a hard laugh, taking a swig from his bottle, his eyes crazed as he pressed his knuckles to the table. "No, it is simply common knowledge."

"You are not more handsome than I," Miles said in a snide voice. "If you admit it to yourself now, you will avoid disappointment. Lady Katherine will choose me. The duke prefers it. We will be the greatest land-owners in the south of England."

Evan's face contorted in vexation. "You always get what you want! It is not fair at all. It is time that I claim something of my own."

Aiden groaned, stepping into the light of the dining room. "Have you considered that Lady Katherine may not wish to marry either of you?"

Evan looked up with a sneer, his eyes bloodshot and dark. "You are only envious of us as you always have been. You will have no opportunity to meet her, and you have nothing, *nothing* that she would desire."

"I have no intention of meeting Lady Katherine. I pity the woman. She will be forced to endure the company of both of you for the evening." Aiden didn't know why he felt the need to rise to the lady's defense, but he couldn't tolerate his stepbrothers any longer, especially when they were so drunk and unaware. He had just turned to walk away when he heard the break-ing of glass crashing against the wall beside him. One of the bottles of brandy.

He whirled around, setting his gaze on Evan who

came to a wobbling stand. "She will be so charmed by me she will be left begging to marry me."

Aiden resisted the urge to laugh. The desperation in his stepbrother's eyes was both pitiful and frightening. "She would never."

Evan dropped down in his chair again. "She might if it will save her reputation." A wicked grin pulled on his mouth, and Aiden had to stop himself from throwing a facer at him.

"You wouldn't dare put her reputation in danger." Anger pounded through him. "That is despicable, even for you."

Evan's temper had transformed into amusement, his words slurred. "There will be other rakes there with similar intentions. I will have to beat them to it. If I ruin her, she will be forced to marry me."

Aiden gritted his teeth. He couldn't fathom such dishonorable behavior. "She will be under careful watch."

"I am skilled at evading the careful chaperones of ladies." Evan came to his feet again, staring at the bottle he had broken with regret, likely wishing he would have drunk it instead. He turned to Aiden. "Clean that up."

Miles stumbled to his feet as well, moving toward the door. Within seconds, the two had disappeared into the dark hallway.

Aiden stood in the dim light, anger pulsing through him with every breath. Surely Lady Katherine's parents understood that there could be wicked men in attendance at their ball. He hoped they had taken the proper precautions. He did not expect the Duke of Chatham to be an imbecile.

"Devil take it," he muttered, bending down to clean up the glass that had shattered all over the ground. If he didn't do it, Lord Aveley would be fit to be tied and send him packing. Aiden couldn't afford that, not now that he was so close to achieving his goal of being a cordwainer.

Worry still thrummed inside him at the idea that Lady Katherine's reputation could be at risk. He could warn Kate on behalf of her mistress. Or he could go to the ball and keep a careful watch on her himself. He pondered over the idea, but quickly stopped himself. Lord Aveley would never allow him to go, especially if he meant to stop Miles and Evan from their opportunity to marry the heiress. But to ruin her reputation as a means to accomplish it? The idea made Aiden's fists curl.

Surely, *surely* she would have another protector there. Several. Who was he to sneak into the ball and keep a careful watch on her? He was merely a friend of her lady's maid, not her guardian or relative.

He rubbed his eyes, excusing his ridiculous thoughts as the result of his lack of sleep. When he finished sweeping the glass into a towel, he carried it carefully to the kitchen to dispose of it. He had been keeping up poorly with cleaning the kitchen, as he was the only one who ever entered it. Lord Aveley had told him that he had conducted interviews with several people from town that were interested in the many open positions in Colborne Hall. Aiden hoped they would begin work soon. As it was, he would still have to stay up for several hours in order to finish the cleaning he had neglected that day, and then he would have to arise early to feed the horses, muck out the stables, prepare breakfast, and countless other responsibilities.

And he desperately wanted to see Kate. He needed to warn her of his stepbrother's intentions toward the heiress.

* * *

Aiden slept an hour, perhaps less, finishing his chores just before dawn. He dragged himself to the center of town, entering the shop.

Mr. Haskett greeted him with a tired smile, yawning as he stretched his back. "Good morning, Notley. You look like death, my friend."

Aiden gave a grim smile, feeling the truth of Mr. Haskett's words in the ache of his muscles and back and the persisting ache in his skull. "If I fell asleep right now you would assume I was dead. I wouldn't awaken for days." He stifled a yawn of his own.

"We cannot have that," Mr. Haskett said. "For we have finally received the orders for Lady Katherine's dancing slippers."

Aiden's eyes widened, even the slight facial expression sending a sharp ache through his forehead. "Have we?"

"Yes. All the details I described before, and a gold satin. They will look very much like your mother's shoes."

Aiden smiled softly. "I have always wanted to create a shoe like hers."

"And so you shall." Mr. Haskett grinned as they both sat down to begin their work. "But there is a slight quandary. We will not be receiving the fabric for several days from a manufacturer in London. So I'm afraid you will have several long nights of work ahead leading up to the ball."

"I look forward to them eagerly."

Mr. Haskett eyed him with disbelief, his keen eyes seemingly surveying every detail of his face. "Return home and rest today. You have been working yourself much too hard."

Aiden paused his work. "I am well enough, I assure you."

"No, you are not. You appear as if you are soon to topple over with exhaustion. Go home now and do not return until dawn tomorrow. I must have you well rested enough to construct Lady Katherine's slippers to the best of your ability. She is an invaluable customer."

Aiden hesitated, but saw in Mr. Haskett's expression an unyielding determination. He would not allow Aiden to take one more stitch.

"Very well," he said. Even as the words escaped him, he came to a full realization of his own exhaustion, feeling the weight of his eyelids and limbs and the ache in his back and fingers. "Thank you, sir. I will return refreshed on the morrow."

Mr. Haskett grunted in approval, continuing his work as Aiden fetched his bag and exited the shop. As much as he longed to sleep in his bed, he knew that if he returned to Colborne Hall he would be pulled into the work that awaited him there. Lord Aveley would never let him rest in the middle of the day. But he could scarcely keep his eyes open.

As he carried himself through the woods, the subtle warmth of the sun filtered through the trees, pulling on his eyelids. He found a warm spot beneath a tree. Using his arm as a pillow, he lay down his head and closed his eyes. The various sounds of the woods calmed him—the chirping of birds, rustling of foliage, buzzing of insects, and the trickle of the brook. His anger toward his stepbrothers was still kindled within him, but it felt more distant as he faded slowly into sleep.

He was resolved to only sleep for an hour or two before returning to Colborne Hall to take advantage of the spare time Mr. Haskett had given him. He was nearly finished preparing the house. As he went through the list of tasks in his mind, he finally fell into a deep and restful sleep.

# Chapter 8

The Duchess of Chatham was more than pleased to have her choice of embellishments for her daughter's gown. Kate listened with half an ear as her mother cheerfully described the Indian paisley that would adorn the hem of her pale blue gown for the ball. Kate had been trapped in the morning room with her mother for nearly two hours that morning, discussing every detail of the ball. The decorations, the ensemble, the food, the company and performances—they were all planned out meticulously. Though she had not met Lord Orsett, her first two dances were already promised to him through her father, with the third belonging to his younger brother, Lord Evan Browning.

When Kate finally managed to escape, she hurried to her room and called Peggy to assist her in changing into one of her simpler morning dresses with a higher hem, one she could easily walk in.

Once she was changed, she sneaked out the back door of Timberwell, escaping across the trimmed lawn toward the woods. The sun was hot today, so she tightened the ribbons of her straw bonnet, knowing the fit her mother would have if she procured a single freckle before the ball. She did not realize how confined she had felt within the walls of Timberwell until she set foot outside. The open freedom of the grasses and surrounding hills inspired her. She breathed in the summer air and set her feet into a run, allowing the wind to whip at her skirts and hair and steal away her breath and worries.

She ran into the trees, enjoying the coolness the shade provided. She kicked the dirt before her, stopping when she saw the silhouette of a man, resting on his side beneath a nearby tree. It took a brief moment before she recognized the mussed dark hair and broad shoulders of Aiden. He wore a tan waistcoat over a white shirt, with dark trousers and boots, the sleeves of his shirt torn at the elbows and stained with dirt. Her heart thudded. Was he well? Why was he lying beneath a tree?

She considered turning back, but worry prevented the action. She walked closer, bending over him to ensure he was well. He appeared only to be sleeping.

His face, pressed into his arm, was serene and handsome. She had always determined it was the color of his eyes that lended his face such handsomeness, but even with them closed, he appeared every bit as hand-

96

some. His dark lashes swept down, his dark brows peaceful and unfurrowed, his mouth relaxed and un-smiling. His hair fell over one side of his forehead.

Kate found herself frozen, studying Aiden's face. The distance between them now—he asleep and she awake—felt very much like the social distance that lay between them. He a servant, she the daughter of a duke. Could such a barrier ever be broken? Sleep could be broken at the drop of a pin, but his station could not be changed.

Why had she not run when she first saw him in the woods? Instead she had pretended to be someone she was not—she had played pretend with a life that was not, and never would be hers. And now all she was left with was cold, stinging regret.

Distracted as she was, she hadn't noticed Aiden shift—not until it was too late. His eyes opened. She concealed her gasp as she leapt behind a nearby tree and pressed her back against the trunk. She held per-fectly still. Perhaps if he had seen her, he would excuse it for his imagination. She held her breath, willing her heart rate to slow as she listened to the leaves rustle with his movement. He was standing, his footfalls crunching closer.

"Kate?" His hushed voice sounded hesitant, but it grew louder. "Kate, is that you?"

She knew there was no sense in hiding a mere three feet away from him. She realized with embarrassment that this was the third time she had been caught hiding from him. Her cheeks burned hot as she stepped away from the tree, facing Aiden's amused grin as he rubbed the sleep from his eyes.

"I am very sorry. I didn't mean to—to..." She couldn't find the words.

"Spy on me?" he chuckled. "Do not be sorry. I am flattered."

She looked up, the width of his smile enough to steal all stability from her knees. His eyes stared intently into hers, the admiration behind them evident. Instant relief and comfort flooded over her, but it was brief, fleeting.

"I must go."

"Please, don't leave." Aiden touched a hand to her elbow, sending a string of shivers over her skin. "You found me at a most opportune time. I have little responsibility for what remains of this day. We might enjoy one another's company a little longer, if you are not otherwise engaged." His voice was soft, innocent, and kind. Kate's legs commanded her to continue walking away, but her heart had other demands.

She turned to face him. The sun came from behind his back, casting her in his shadow. The warmth of his closeness and his smiling eyes forced her decision. "I am not otherwise engaged." She swallowed. "My mistress is out today, so I will not be missed."

His smile reminded her of a young boy, cheerful without reservation, light and free of pretense. "Would you walk with me?" He extended his arm, the torn sleeve reminding her yet again of the danger of growing too close to him. But she was tired—so tired of succumbing to the demands of her station and her parents. Could she not claim something for her own happiness?

In answer, she wrapped her hand around his elbow. "Yes."

They began walking, ducking past low-hanging branches and stepping over roots that crossed the path. It was unlike any walk Kate had ever taken with a gentleman in the gardens of Silverbard or the parks in London. There were no neat grasses and perfect hedges to be found.

"What brought you to the woods today?" Aiden's voice came strong and deep, breaking through the quiet surroundings. "I can't assume I would be so fortunate to have been your only reason for venturing here."

She turned her face up to look at him, noting the smiling creases near his eyes. She longed to tell him everything, to confide in him her worries over the upcoming ball, of the fortune hunters that would be in attendance, of her father's list of suitable gentlemen that did not include Aiden. But as she stared into his eyes, her words halted in her throat. "I needed to escape, if even for a moment."

Worry immediately furrowed his brow. "Escape?"

She shook her head. "It is nothing so dire. I simply find that I am trapped by my circumstances. Circumstances that others would view as freedom, I feel quite caged by."

"I know how it feels to long for escape." His voice grew quiet. "We may not be in control of our circumstances, but we are in control of our reaction to them. We control how deeply they penetrate us. One might view misfortune as a gift, as it allows you to treasure much more each fortunate thing that befalls you." He stopped to grip her hand. Her eyes flew up to his face. "You, Kate. I treasure you. I—I believe I may be falling in love with you."

The sweetness of his words ached in her chest. Her heart hammered against her ribcage, another cage with which she was bound. Her heart could never escape its duty. It could never belong to him.

"Mr. Notley," she shook her head at the ground, tearing her gaze from his face. "I have not been entirely honest with you." Heat rose to her cheeks with the increase of her pulse. How could she confess to her lies? To do so would be the most difficult thing she had ever done. "I have neglected to tell you…" She paused. Would it be so very bad to hold onto her ruse for one more day? "… that you have become a very dear friend." Her words came out rushed, too quick to sound sincere.

Aiden released her hand, his own cheeks reddening at the centers. "A friend?" He nodded. "Forgive me, Miss Kate, if I have spoken too freely."

She shook her head. "Not at all." Her heart still thrummed against her chest with his words. "You are very kind."

He drew a deep breath, a smile lighting his features. "I am glad you found me here. I've been given the day off and was hoping to somehow spend it with you."

She couldn't believe that she had come across him in the woods. It was as if fate were playing her hand to throw them together. But how could that be so? His eyes had their usual effect on her thoughts, sending them spinning in irrational directions. She stooped below a bare branch, misjudging the distance. The branch caught a strand of her hair, causing her to stop abruptly. She laughed, struggling to pull away.

Aiden jumped to action, turning toward her, extending his hands above her head to free her hair from the branch. His fingers brushed against her skin. His chin was level with her eyes, and she could feel the faintness of his breath against her forehead, see the steady rise and fall of his chest as he untangled her hair. Her laughter grew soft, strained against the beating of her heart.

When he finished, he smoothed the curls back from her eyes, smiling down at her with enough admiration to set her legs shaking. What would it be like to kiss him? She had never kissed a man, though more than one had attempted to kiss her. She had been the victim of two different men that had attempted to be caught with her in a compromising situation, hoping to reap the rewards of a marriage with her through such unscrupulous ways. But she knew Aiden was not such a man. He would not steal a kiss from her—he would wait until it was willingly given. He would wait, he would cherish her, he would not care about her fortune more than he cared about her. She had learned to defend herself against wicked men, and she knew how to sense them coming. Aiden was the kindest, most sincere and good man she had had ever met. She could trust him—she could even trust him enough to allow him to kiss her.

He looked into her eyes, the distance between them growing smaller. His gaze dropped to her lips, his breathing falling out of rhythm. Her own breath stalled as he touched her cheek.

"I believe I set you free from the branch," he said, his voice low and hoarse. He smiled, breaking the enchantment that seemed to have fallen between them. He gestured at the branch above, and she forced a laugh, taking a step away from him.

"Thank you. You have rescued me on more than one occasion." Her smile grew with his—a smile so wide her cheeks ached. "Freddy is still under punishment. He will be quite envious that I have the privilege of seeing you and he does not."

He laughed, shaking his head. "My company isn't such a novelty."

"It is," she protested. "I—I have never felt more myself than when I am with you. You have a certain ease of character that is quite infectious."

He looked down at the ground with her compliment, his humility evident. All her suitors that would

102

come calling to Silverbard reveled in her flattery, false as it was.

"I should hate to have you feel anything but ease around me." He met her eyes. "I hope there is nothing that would deter you from spending time with me."

Guilt writhed in her stomach, nearly choking her. There were many things that could deter her from seeing him again, especially after the ball. She would be faced with many potential husbands there, and her parents would expect her to pursue them.

When she failed to answer, he took another step away, leaving the shade of the tree. "There is a matter I must warn you of in behalf of your mistress." His expression grew serious.

Dread fell through her. "What is it?"

"As you know, I work in the home of Lord Aveley and his sons. I overheard them speaking of their intentions toward Lady Katherine. I'm afraid Evan—Lord Browning intends to ruin her reputation as an attempt to gain her hand in marriage."

Kate's heart raced. Any hope she had held that Lord Evan Browning would be a desirable match fled her. Was Lord Orsett her only hope? If his brother was such a scoundrel, he could very well be the same. She slumped against the tree, her muscles growing weak. She didn't even know the appearance of Lord Aveley or his sons, and she wouldn't until they were introduced. If she told her father of Aiden's warning, he would dismiss it. He would never trust the word of a servant above the marquess who had spoken highly of his sons.

"Will Lady Katherine have adequate protection at the ball? Will the duke be keeping a careful watch on her?"

Kate nodded. "She will know to be wary of Lord Aveley and his sons." She swallowed. "Thank you for warning me. I will—I will pass the warning to her."

He did not seem to be convinced. He studied her with a look of deep examination. "Are you certain? If it is possible, I will find a way to the ball myself and keep careful watch of the marquess's son."

Gratitude welled in her chest, mingling with the longing she had felt for him to attend the ball. She would feel safe with him near. She would finally have a reason not to dread the ball. But how could he attend? He would see her there and know she had been lying to him. He would know that she was the duke's daughter, the one he had come to protect.

"She will be fine. I will ensure her protection myself. At any rate, you would not be able to enter the ball, being a servant." Her voice softened and she looked down at her feet.

When she looked up at him again, a muscle jumped in his clenched jaw. He looked as if he wished to say more, but stopped himself. "Very well, but please remember that these men are cunning. They want nothing more than Lady Katherine's fortune, and they will go to despicable lengths to obtain it."

Another surge of fear struck her chest. "I understand. I will instruct her to take care."

He nodded, reaching inside his boot to withdraw a small pocket watch. The outside was carved intricately with doves. He opened it to check the time before snapping it closed. He smiled at the contraption, a certain wistful longing in his expression.

"This belonged to my father." He held the watch up to the light. "It was my mother's before that. She gave it to him as a gift at their engagement."

She smiled, the fear within her fading with his sentiments. "Are your parents well?"

He shook his head. "They died several years ago. First my father, then my mother."

Kate felt his grief, stinging in her own heart. She was reminded yet again of how very fortunate she was. She had both her parents still living, caring for her happiness.

"You must miss them terribly."

He gave a soft smile. "I do miss them, but I see them in the things they left behind. I see my father in this watch. I see him in my own reflection, and in the sound of my own voice. I see my mother in the trees and flowers, and in the dancing slippers she left behind." He looked down, becoming shy once again. "I see a bit of her in you as well. In your kindness and joyful disposition." He met her eyes, and it was all she could do not to cry. How could Aiden be more genuine and sweet? Her heart ached.

"Your parents sound lovely," she whispered. "I'm certain you house many more qualities of theirs than even you realize."

"I hope one day to be like them." He squared his shoulders, his determination evident.

The air between them fell silent, and he extended his arm to her again. She took it, comfortable in the serene sounds of nature as they walked. They followed the path of the brook, and Aiden teased her about her fall, and they laughed until their stomachs ached. For hours they talked and laughed and teased. Kate had never been more content.

Her grief threatened to overwhelm her as the sun faded below the horizon and he bid her farewell. He walked her to the edge of the Timberwell property, but not farther. She could only imagine her mother's anger when she arrived after having been gone the entire day without explanation.

Aiden took her hand in his, placing a gentle kiss against it. "Extend my greetings to Freddy," he said, keeping her hand wrapped up in his.

"I will." A tear slipped from her eye as she turned, but the darkness concealed it from his view. "Goodbye, Mr. Notley."

"Goodbye." His voice was cheerful, light, a stark contrast to the emotion that burned in her heart.

The permanence of that goodbye would haunt her forever. She could not face him again. To do so would be foolish and would only hurt them both. She was tempted to run again, but she maintained her pace, stepping over the grass while tears fell silently down her cheeks.

# Chapter 9

A week had passed since Aiden had last seen Kate. Memories of their last meeting still thrived in his mind, filling him with strength and resolve. Once he had a secure living in place, he could ask her to marry him. He had never been more certain of anything in his life. He wanted to have many more days with Kate like he had just had the week before.

He had been busy all week working on Lady Katherine's shoes, day and night, as well as finishing the cleaning of Colborne Hall. He had walked through the woods, hoping to find Kate there, but he had been unsuccessful. He stopped himself from worrying over her, focusing on the task at hand. The slippers were nearly complete. He poked at the fire in the cordwainer's shop, the dim light becoming a strain on his vision. The flames grew, and he returned to his wooden stool.

The duke and duchess had begun to grow impatient. Mr. Haskett had assured them the slippers would arrive in time for the ball, but Aiden was beginning to doubt himself. The ball was the next day, and he would need to deliver them promptly in the morning.

He had overheard his stepbrothers speaking again of their intentions toward Lady Katherine, and Aiden had half a mind to rush to Timberwell and warn the duke and duchess himself. But surely Kate had warned her mistress of the danger Miles and Evan presented. He pushed away his troubled thoughts.

He had finished the fabric rosettes that would adorn the toes of the slippers, and was now finishing the structure of the silk shoe. By the time the sun rose, Mr. Haskett returned to the shop, and Aiden was still not finished.

Aiden stretched his back with a sigh of frustration, the slippers still not nearly as perfect as he wanted them to be. Mr. Haskett's cheeks reddened with concealed anxiety, picking up one of the slippers carefully.

"They are nearly finished," Aiden said.

"Not so." Mr. Haskett fanned his face with one hand, drying the perspiration that had gathered on his forehead. "The sole has yet to be attached, and the rosettes are still resting on the table." He puffed a long breath out from his nostrils. "Will they be finished in time for the ball?"

"Yes. I assure you, they will." Aiden squared his shoulders and returned his wearied focus to the slippers.

Mr. Haskett still appeared hesitant, but he walked

away, his breathing still quickened with worry. "We cannot lose the duchess as a customer," he muttered, more to himself than to Aiden.

Aiden stared out the front window of the shop. He had to finish the slippers in time for the ball. His stepfather had also requested that he finish polishing the silver in the dining room that day for his upcoming guests. And all Aiden could think about was his next opportunity to see Kate. Perhaps when he delivered the shoes to Timberwell he could request to see her, but she still thought him to be a mere servant in Colborne Hall. She didn't know he was working to become a tradesman, or that he was the son of a gentleman.

He cringed inwardly at the depth of lies he had found himself in. Why had he not simply confessed his true position to her? Why had he allowed his stepfather to dictate yet another aspect of his life? His ruse would end tonight. He needed to confess.

When the sun reached its highest point in the sky, Aiden still was not finished. As it faded toward the horizon, he still was not finished. And as night fell upon Gravesend, he finally took his last stitch, securing the last rosette to the top of the slipper. Mr. Haskett had been practically hovering over him as he worked, pacing in circles of anticipation.

"How extraordinary," the strained compliment had come multiple times, always ending with a huffed and exerted breath.

The ball was only minutes from beginning.

"Please, let me inspect them." Mr. Haskett snatched the shoes from Aiden's grasp, studying them from every angle. "Very well, very well done." His brows drew together above his spectacles. "They could not be more well made, Notley. If only you had finished them faster. Only a shoe this lovely could tempt the duchess to remain a customer of ours after such late delivery. Make haste!" He clapped his hands together. "Take them to Timberwell at once! The ball is beginning at nine!"

Aiden checked his pocket watch, dismayed by the sight. He had thirty minutes to make it inside Timberwell before they began welcoming their guests. He jumped from his stool, dizzy from the sudden movement.

"Oh, blast. You look positively dreadful. I will not have a representative of mine arrive at the home of a duke appearing so rugged."

"I must hurry, sir—"

"It will be but a moment." Mr. Haskett hustled out the door of the shop, returning shortly with the modiste from the shop next door. "Madam Boisseau has agreed to lend you a set of proper clothing. The woman beside him held a silver waistcoat, black jacket, and fitted trousers over her arm.

Her sharp eyes took in his appearance. She tsked when she saw his hair. "Sit." Her commanding voice gave Aiden no choice but to listen. She pulled a comb from her apron pocket and ran it swiftly through his dark hair. She thrust the stack of clothing toward Mr. Haskett, beckoning them both to follow her to her neighboring shop.

The place was empty, dress forms and fabrics hanging all around. "My seamstresses have retired for the evening," she said over her shoulder. "They have been worn to the bone with the making of Lady Katherine's gown, just as you have with her slippers. She ought to be a pretty girl if such expenses are to be made on her behalf. Have you seen her?"

It took a moment for Aiden to realize that Madam Boisseau addressed him. "No, I have not."

"Hmm." She pulled him toward a sheeted dressing room. "Now, I suspect these will fit, but you must try them first. Mr. Haskett, do assist him with his cravat." She addressed Aiden. "The way you present yourself will affect us all. We cannot have you reflecting badly on the Gravesend shops."

"Certainly not." Mr. Haskett nodded.

Aiden changed quickly into the clothes. The snug and perfect fit of the jacket and trousers was astonishing. He stepped out from the curtain, earning a gasp of delight from Madam Boisseau. "Perfection!"

She thrust the piece of silken white fabric toward Mr. Haskett, commissioning him to tie it elaborately at Aiden's neck. Aiden raised his chin to allow room for the cravat. He had never worn more than a simple knot, yet he had tied many more elaborate ones on his stepbrothers.

"There. I would be pleased to present you for the queen."

"How very handsome you are, Mr. Notley." Madam Boisseau circled him, eyes round with approval. "Take care to mention my hand in your clothing if compliments are to be received."

He laughed, uncomfortable with the attention. "You may rely upon it. I could never claim such finery as my own."

She laughed, a somewhat flirtatious sound. "Oh, Mr. Notley. It is your natural assets that bring your appearance such advantage. A well-dressed man cannot live up to a handsome and kind one."

"The time! The slippers!" Mr. Haskett had been staring at Aiden as a father might stare proudly at a son, forgetting the most important matter at hand. Aiden followed him out of the shop and took the boxed slippers under his arm.

"Make haste, Notley!" Mr. Haskett shouted as Aiden set off on foot toward Timberwell. Madam Boisseau waved at him, a bright smile on her cheeks.

Aiden checked his pocket watch again, moving his feet faster across the dark cobblestones. He knew the way to Timberwell without hesitation, and he arrived in less than twenty minutes. Carriages had already arrived on the drive, their inhabitants waiting impatiently to be invited inside. He arrived at the front door, jumping over the steps. He raised the brass knocker and waited.

The butler pulled the door open, taking in his appearance with curiosity.

"Good evening, sir. I am here on delivery of Lady Katherine's slippers. On behalf of Mr. Haskett, I offer my sincere apology for the lack of punctuality. We—"

A young woman stepped up beside the butler, eyeing the box with a flick of her gaze. "Are those m'lady's slippers?"

Aiden felt his brow contract. "Yes. I thought I might deliver them to Lady Katherine's maid."

"I'm her maid, sir." The young woman grasped impatiently at the box, offering him a curt smile. "She mustn't be late for her own ball."

"Does Lady Katherine have another maid? One by the name of Kate?"

The young woman's cheeks paled and she shook her head. "I'm 'fraid not. Good evening, sir." She bustled toward the staircase, taking one more glance at him over her shoulder.

Aiden took a step back, offering a polite bow. Confusion tore through him. The butler stepped aside to welcome a new throng of guests into the entry hall, and Aiden moved to allow them entrance. He retreated down the steps, his mind racing.

A familiar carriage rode past, and he averted his face, knowing it to be his stepfather's carriage. He circled around the side of the house, watching as Lord Aveley and Evan descended from the coach. He waited for Miles to emerge, but he was not among them.

Evan grinned triumphantly as he walked over the grass. Aiden was close enough to the front entrance to hear them.

Lord Aveley was greeted by a woman that could only be the duchess, regally dressed with perfect posture. He bowed. "I regret to inform you that my eldest son, the Earl of Orsett was unable to attend this evening. He is not well, I'm afraid." His voice was strained, and Aiden caught the suppressed grin on Evan's face.

It would not surprise Aiden in the slightest if he found that Evan had been responsible for Miles's *being unwell* that evening.

The two men entered the house, disappearing among the crowd of eager guests. Aiden could not help but notice that most of the guests were young men, as if the duke and duchess had designed this ball in an attempt to find a husband for their daughter. How many would have sinister motivations similar to Evan's?

Aiden's heart sunk at the suspicion that had been on his mind since the moment he had first met Kate. He had met the heiress's maid tonight, and it was not her. Could she have lied about her position in the household? Could she not be a maid at all?

He thought of her fine dresses and clear skin and soft hands. Her refined voice and manners. He had suspected it, but he had been given no reason to doubt Kate's word. The truth of it now seemed so obvious.

She was the duke's daughter. She was the heiress of Silverbard—the one Evan planned to force into marriage.

A surge of emotions entered Aiden's chest—anger at Evan's intentions and Kate's deception, disappointment, fear, worry. He stepped away from his place at the side of the house and took stride across the grass, purpose in his steps. He approached amid a crowd of guests, reaching the duchess. She blanched when he attempted to walk past without introduction.

"I do not believe we have met." Her eyes took him in with curiosity, falling upon his fine attire and returning to his face.

"I come from Colborne Hall, your grace." Lord Aveley would murder him if he confessed to be his stepson and not merely a servant. Before he could explain his identity, the duchess's face ignited with pleasure, her smile wide and her cheeks flushed. "Oh, Lord Orsett, you are most welcome here. I must confess myself surprised at your arrival. Your father claimed you were unwell."

Aiden froze, a denial hovering on his lips. His eyes shifted to the ballroom, where he caught a glimpse of Evan, a satisfied sneer on his lips as he surveyed the crowd. Aiden could not leave Kate to face Evan alone.

He cleared his throat. "I was only a trifle ill, your grace. I could not miss the opportunity to be acquainted with your daughter."

"Oh, I am very glad you have come." The duchess motioned for him to enter, whispering his name to the footman that would announce his entrance to the crowded ballroom. As he drew closer to the ballroom doors, he searched the crowd for any sight of Lord Aveley and Evan. If he was introduced as Lord Orsett his ruse would end before it had even begun. Was there an alternate entrance he could take? His heart pounded hard against his chest as he approached.

Lord Aveley and Evan stood on the opposite side of the ballroom. With guests being announced continuously, it was possible they could miss his introduction. Both men were engaged in conversation when the footman announced Aiden's entrance.

"His lordship, the Earl of Orsett."

Aiden stepped swiftly away from the doorway, one eye fixed on his stepfather and Evan. They did not look up from their conversation, the nearby music and chatter enough to disguise the footman's loud, albeit inferior voice.

Aiden breathed a sigh of relief as he found a place behind a crowd of men, avoiding being seen by his stepfather. He noticed several eyes upon him, a challenge in the gaze of almost every gentleman he passed. Only then did he see Kate—or rather, Lady Katherine, standing alone on the outskirts of the ballroom. A man who, by his air of superiority, could only be the duke, stood at her side, seemingly intent to introduce her to every man in the room.

Miss Kate was the duke's daughter. Here was his proof.

And now both she and the duke stared across the room at Aiden, who they supposed to be Lord Orsett. He froze.

What had he done?

# Chapter 10

Kate blinked to clear her vision, her ears ringing with the sound of the footman's name as he had announced Lord Orsett. She had turned toward the door at the announcement, and despite her mother's every instruction of keeping a proper expression at all times, her jaw had dropped.

It must have been a mistake. Aiden could not have been Lord Orsett. But his appearance—his fine clothing and combed hair and handsome brown eyes staring across the room at her showed every sign of nobility. Had he truly been pretending, just as she had, to be someone else? But why had he warned her to beware of Lord Aveley's sons? He was one of them.

Her heart hammered against the tight stays that had been laced around her lungs, the long train of her gown brushing against the ballroom floor as she approached him. She wanted to be angry that he had

deceived her, but how could she? She had done the
same to him.

Relief so strong flooded through her body, bringing
a smile of wonder and awe to her cheeks. Her father
held her back by the elbow. "Not so fast, my dear." He
gave a low chuckle. "I must introduce you. I have not
yet been acquainted with the young earl myself."

She stopped her advance, her cheeks hot. Her father
approached him before ushering Kate forward. "May I
present my daughter, Lady Katherine Golding."

Kate's heart thudded as she met Aiden's eyes. He
had never looked more handsome. His eyes shone under the flames that lit the ballroom as he stared back at
her. She wanted to speak with him privately, to explain
why she had lied to him, to inquire after why he had
lied to her. She felt a misunderstanding still hanging
between them, tightening the air with unanswered
questions.

"It is a pleasure to meet you, Lord Orsett." Kate
dropped her head in a bow, her limbs shaking. She met
his eyes, prodding him with her gaze. What reason
could he have had to pretend to be a servant? Did he
have the same reasons she had? She could not think of
him by any other name but Aiden. But was that even
his true Christian name?

"As promised, I have reserved my daughter's first
two dances for you." Kate's father addressed the earl.
"The first set is to begin shortly."

Chagrin flushed Aiden's cheeks, and he gave a nod.

"Yes, of course."

Kate's father spoke again in a cheerful voice. "Why did you not arrive with Lord Aveley and your brother?"

"They assumed I was not well enough to come." He cleared his throat, his expression somewhat panicked as he looked across the room at who she assumed was Lord Aveley and Lord Evan Browning.

Kate's stomach turned when she saw the son, his ghostly white skin and black hair, his sneering red lips as he surveyed the crowd. Her worries ceased when she looked at Aiden. He would not allow any harm to befall her. She felt even more safe beside him than her own father. Her father was far too trusting of men of high birth. Aiden knew enough of his own brother's character to know that he meant trouble. Aiden gave a tight smile. "But I am well enough."

"Indeed." Kate's father studied him for a long moment as, to her relief, the music began with new vigor.

"Go, enjoy the dance!" her father ushered the couple forward, and Kate stepped into line across from Aiden. Every eye in the room watched her—watched Aiden. How could they speak of their deception here, in front of so many watchful people? Her heart thudded as the first steps of the dance brought them together, their hands touching briefly before breaking apart.

"Aiden," she whispered as she drew near to him once again. Tears suddenly burned behind her eyes. "I am sorry," she breathed.

She followed the steps of the dance as they carried her away, and back again. "I should not have lied to you. But I can see now that you have pretended to be a servant as well."

His jaw was firm, his eyes searching hers. "I did pretend. But not in the way you assume. I am a servant of a sort."

The suspense tightened her muscles as she moved away, coming back again. He gripped her hand in his. "I am not who you believe me to be." He looked at the nearby couples, who were quite obvious in their attempts to overhear the conversation.

"Then who are you?" she whispered.

"No one of consequence."

"All people are of consequence."

She circled around him, their hands lightly touching, the warmth threading down her arm and touching her heart with uncertainty.

"I came to ensure no harm could befall you." He leaned close to her ear as he passed. "Forgive me, but my identity was mistaken upon my entrance."

Her heart fell and a new surge of emotion gripped her throat. "You are not the earl?"

He gave a subtle shake of his head, a rueful movement that brought melancholy to her bones. "Then who are you?" she repeated, careful to hide the desperation in her voice. The hope she had felt was quickly fading. It would have been too fortuitous for him to truly be Lord Orsett. Too good to be true.

The song ended, and they bowed to each other. He walked forward, his eyes flashing. "I will explain it all to you, but I cannot do so here. My ruse will be discovered soon." He looked to the right, where Lord Aveley and his son stared, mouths agape and eyes heavy with anger. They were connected to him somehow, Kate could clearly decipher. Perhaps he was their servant after all. Her heart sank.

"Will you be punished for coming here, for interfering with Lord Evan's scheme?" Her voice shook.

He grasped her hand. "Do not worry over me."

"But I cannot help it." She wanted to speak the words that hung on her lips, that pounded in her throat. She cared for him deeply, more than she had ever cared for anyone. She couldn't bear the thought of never seeing him again.

He gave her a soft smile, squeezing her hand before releasing it. The crowd watched the exchange intently, Kate's father with deep pleasure. When he discovered that Aiden was not Lord Orsett, he would be furious.

"Does Lord Aveley know that you pretended to be his son?"

"No." Aiden shook his head. "But he will discover the truth soon enough. It is obvious he is not pleased to see me here."

"So you cannot stay?" She wanted to cling to his arm, to run away from the stifling ballroom and away from her father's expectations. From the corner of her eye, she saw Lord Evan approaching with long strides.

His father followed close behind. "The gardens," she blurted. "I will be in the gardens."

She met Aiden's eyes quickly, the confirmation in them evident as she pulled away from his side. As she hurried past her father, she muttered, "I feel unwell."

His protest was muffled by the surrounding voices as she pushed through the crowd, cursing her thick petticoat and long skirts as she brushed through the doorway. The slippers she wore fit perfectly, soft and light, the one comfortable piece of clothing she had been allowed to wear to the ball. Her feet carried her lightly across the marble floors and out the back door of the house. She turned to the left, entering the intricate maze of shrubbery and flowers.

When she was sufficiently hidden, she sat down on a stone bench, her breath quick with the exertion of her swift escape, and the fear that came at the prospect of the punishment that would await Aiden.

And herself.

She put her face in her hands, reminding her of the day she had been sitting in the gardens of Silverbard, plagued by the presence of Mr. Boyle. His high-pitched voice entered her mind, the memory jarring.

It took the briefest of moments for her to realize that the voice she heard did not come from a memory. Her shoulders jerked up, her face flying out from the cover of her hands. In the dark shadow of a hedge, hidden from the moonlight, came the voice again.

"You look positively ravishing this evening, my lady."

A chill touched the back of her neck, an icy grip coming over her limbs. It was not Aiden. "Who are you?"

A chuckle, more of a masculine giggle, came through the breezy air. "A man of great consequence."

She moved slowly to her feet as the figure of Lord Evan Browning appeared in the darkness. She swallowed, sickening dread pooling in her stomach. "Sir, we have not been introduced. I—"

"Come now, you do not seem intent on following the rules of society." He stepped closer, the milky whiteness of his skin making stark contrast with his dark eyes and crimson lips. His mouth stretched into a smile, his crooked teeth making a startling appearance. "You danced the last set with a servant, after all." His giggle came again, louder, with a note of frustration. "A servant of my household." His feet carried him closer, and she backed away from the bench. "What did he tell you? Hmm? Did he flatter you into believing he cared for you? It is a skill he possesses. Did he tell you he was not such a servant? Did he claim a relation to my family?"

She narrowed her eyes at him. "Pray, sir, do not come a step closer."

He stopped his approach, a wild sneer of amusement on his face. "You would let a servant close but not a gentleman?"

"A servant that behaves as a gentleman should, is much better than a gentleman who behaves like a rogue." She snapped the words at him, holding her chin high despite the fear that trembled her legs.

He tipped his head back, laughing up at the moon. "Ah, my lady, you have been deceived. The man you claim to be a gentleman has nothing in his sight but your fortune. He hopes to climb the ranks of society and escape his life of poverty. That is his only design upon you."

She did not believe a word of it. She had learned how to sort out the fortune hunters. Aiden was not one of them. He met her as Miss Kate, knowing nothing of her fortune. He was honorable, good, and kind. Lord Evan Browning, however, was not.

"I believe you speak of yourself," she said. "Now, please return to the ballroom and leave me."

His amusement was fading quickly, replaced with hot anger. She stepped back fast, unwilling to turn her back on him. Her heart raced with fear as her back crashed against a shrub. He took advantage of her immobility, lunging forward and clasping her upper arm in his grip. She cried out, but he covered her mouth with one hand.

His dark eyes glistened inches from hers, desperation to the point of madness within them. "You will enter my carriage without a sound. We will made a dash for Scotland, where we will elope. If you do not comply, I will ensure that Aiden Notley has the most miserable life it is in my power to give him. My father will ensure the same."

126

She tried to shake her head as tears streamed down her cheeks, but he held her face tightly. "Not a sound, my dear."

She gritted her teeth, her pulse pounding in her ears. Where was Aiden? It had been several minutes since she had escaped to the gardens. Surely he would be coming soon. She simply needed to delay. But how?

"Do we have an accord?" He pinched her face between his hand, pulling her closer. When she refused to answer, he repeated, his voice lowering, "*Do we have an accord?*"

Her eyes darted in every direction, her ears straining to hear any sign that Aiden was coming. But all she heard were crickets and the raspy breathing of Evan.

"Make haste with your answer, or I will both marry you and make Aiden's life miserable."

She forced a breath through her nostrils, tearing her face away from his hand. "Yes," she said in a hard voice.

"Very well." He hesitantly released the weight of his grip on her arm, wrapping her hand gently around his elbow. He began walking, and panic rose in her throat. How could she escape? There was not another person in sight among the gardens, and the house was growing farther and farther away. Even her screams would not be heard.

"Wait," she blurted.

His quick steps did not halt, and he tightened his grip on her arm. "There is no time to waste."

She took one more desperate glance over her shoulder, regret and fear battling for dominance within her. Would Aiden find her in time?

A gig, hidden among the trees behind the house, awaited them with a single horse. She considered running, but her layers of skirts and length of the train would not allow it. But that could not stop her from trying. She tore her arm away from him, gathered her skirts in her hands, and ran in the direction of the house. He caught her within seconds, pulling her roughly toward him. Tears slipped from her eyes as he dragged her toward the gig. One of her slippers had fallen off in the struggle. It shone in the moonlit grass, solitary and beautiful, despite the terrifying dread that hummed in the air. She stared at the gold satin fabric, the image blurred behind her liquid eyes.

"You will be wise to not try that again." Lord Evan's disturbingly high voice came close to her ear, his wet breath against it. All she could do was comply and hope—pray that they would be discovered.

Lord Evan gripped her at the waist, lifting her into the gig, his hands lingering there. He grinned up at her, his white hand reaching to stroke her cheek. She turned her face away in disgust.

"Come now, you are to be my wife. You mustn't shy away from my touch forever."

She shuddered, crossing her arms, the dread intensifying in her stomach. She felt she might be ill. Could she jump from the gig and make a dash for the house?

If she screamed loud enough she would possibly be heard by one of the footmen outside. But if she did not comply, then Lord Evan would ensure a life of misery from Aiden. She could never aid in securing him such a fate. Love required sacrifice. Aiden had risked so much in coming to the ball to protect her. A knot formed in her throat.

But where was he now?

The reins flicked over the horse's back, and the wheels began turning. Kate watched Timberwell in forced silence until she and Lord Evan became engulfed in the trees.

# Chapter 11

The moment Kate had left Aiden's side, Lord Aveley took her place, the anger in his voice unconcealed as he beckoned Aiden to the dark hallway. Aiden followed reluctantly, searching the crowd for Evan. He could not see him.

"What the devil are you doing here?" Lord Aveley half-shouted once they were away from the assembly. "You are not to claim any relation to my family. You are a servant in my house! Everyone will wonder why I have been hiding my *stepson*." He said the word as if it tasted of stale tea. "They will look upon me with disdain."

Aiden did not want to know what his stepfather would do if he confessed that he had claimed to be Lord Orsett, his own son, upon his entrance. If his stepfather discovered the deception he would likely send Aiden to the streets.

Aiden glared at him. "They will look upon you with more disdain if they learn that you have been conspiring with your sons to ruin the reputation of Lady Katherine in an attempt to secure a marriage with her."

Lord Aveley sputtered. "You cannot prove that."

Intense worry filled Aiden as he surveyed the ballroom again, failing to find Evan among the guests. Kate had gone to the gardens to await Aiden. Could Evan have followed her?

The thought sent a chill of dread through him. He tightened his fists. "I must go."

"Go where?" his stepfather spat. "If you think you are going to win the hand of the heiress you are mistaken. It will not be long before Evan meets success."

The duke stepped out from the nearby ballroom, striding toward Aiden and his stepfather.

"Your grace," Lord Aveley dropped a bow.

The duke nodded briefly in return, turning his attention to Aiden. "Orsett, do you know where my daughter has gone? After your dance she fled from the ballroom." His expression was dark, protective.

Lord Aveley sputtered again. "Orsett?"

Aiden ignored him. "She mentioned the gardens. But I fear she may be in danger. I will go in search of her now."

The duke gave him a look of confusion, worry of his own tightening his brow. "Pray tell, in danger of what?"

131

Aiden could not wait another moment. He ran down the dark hallway, leaving the astonished duke and his stepfather. Aiden's pulse rushed past his ears as he stormed through the dark hallways in search of the back door. The gardens. *Where were the blasted gardens?* Where was the back door?

He rounded a hall to the right, throwing open a small door near the back of the house. As soon as it opened, Freddy came flying out from what turned out to be a closet, his claws sliding across the marble floors as he barked. The dog jumped up on Aiden's legs, his hostility turning playful.

"We must find Kate," Aiden said, beckoning the dog to follow him. He found the back door and threw it open, letting Freddy free into the night.

"Kate!" he called, not bothering to whisper. The dread in his stomach prevented it; the feeling would not abandon him. He feared the worst. "Kate!"

He ran around to the gardens, jogging between shrubs and dark, flowering bushes, the dog close at his heels. He looked behind the various stone fountains, finding no sign of her. He ran across the back lawn. Had she even come to the gardens at all? Or had Evan led her elsewhere? He couldn't believe she would go willingly. She knew from Aiden's warning that Evan was dangerous.

Far across the grass, near the line of the woods, something gold caught his eye. He ran toward it, his heart sinking when he realized what it was.

A slipper.

The slipper he had made for her, abandoned in the grass. Freddy leapt toward it, sniffing the gold silk before turning his face up to the trees with a growl.

Aiden's heart thudded hard against his chest, his gaze frantic as he searched the surrounding area. He noticed a deep imprint of wheels marking the grass at the edge of the woods.

Had Evan abducted her? They could not have travelled far in the time it had taken him to escape his stepfather's side. Without another thought, Aiden tore through the trees and onto the path, running as quickly as his well-tailored clothing would allow, the dog leading the way.

\* \* \*

Kate heard a familiar sound, one that took her a moment to comprehend. She jerked upright, the sound too faint and distant to believe.

Could it be Freddy's bark?

She strained her ears, struggling to hear the sound over the revolutions of the wheels through the twigs and leaves on the wooded path.

Lord Evan held the reins tightly beside her, flicking them constantly, sending the poor horse into a strained trot. She steadied her breathing, trying to appear nonchalant as she glanced behind them.

"What are you looking for?" Lord Evan questioned

with a lazy smile. "We have evaded all notice. You will not escape this marriage."

Kate could hear the tremor of doubt in his voice. His dark eyes surveyed every angle of their surroundings, shifting with unease. He urged the horse to move faster.

Kate gave a silent gasp as the sound she had been listening to grew closer. It was definitely Freddy. But how had he escaped? She turned in her seat, squinting through the darkness. The color of Freddy's coat would be difficult to discern in the darkness, but she would try. Hope sparked in her chest when the sound of heavier footfalls behind the barking—the breaking of twigs underfoot—reached her ears.

"Make haste, you stupid beast," Lord Evan snarled, whipping the horse across the back. The gig jerked forward, moving dangerously fast over the path. The conveyance teetered back and forth, wild desperation returning to Lord Evan's eyes.

Still watching the ground behind her, Kate caught sight of a flash of gray fur, followed by a set of shiny black boots, dark trousers, and a silver waistcoat. Aiden.

Without thinking, she grasped at the reins in Lord Evan's hands, her movement quick and unsuspected. The reins slipped from his hands and she pulled them tight, bringing the horse to a slow stop. Lord Evan snarled, attempting to wrestle them back from her. Her fight against him only lasted a short moment be-

fore the reins were in his control again. But not before
Freddy caught up to the gig, leaping onto the narrow
step and into Lord Evan's lap with a surprisingly deep
growl.

Lord Evan screamed, attempting to throw Freddy
from his lap, but Freddy's teeth had made a secure hold
on his forearm. Kate gasped as he managed to detach
her dog, sending him flying off the gig. Aiden caught
him before he could hit the ground.

She found his gaze, tears pouring from her eyes all
over again. His previously neat hair had fallen over his
brow, his chest rising and falling quickly. His eyes only
lingered on her for a moment, and she felt safe. Secure.

His eyes hardened like steel when he turned them
on Lord Evan. He handed Freddy to Kate before
rounding the gig and taking a fistful of Lord Evan's
jacket, pulling him out of the gig with great force.

Kate hugged Freddy to her chest, her heart racing
like a trapped bird against his little body.

Lord Evan did not appear afraid, not even a little.
He laughed, his dark hair falling in black feathers on
his forehead. "You would try to stop me, stepbrother?
You think anyone will trust your word above mine or
my father's? If we are discovered, I will claim it was
*you* who abducted the heiress. Who will he believe?
Hmm?"

Aiden shoved him back against the gig. "Did you
hurt her?"

Lord Evan laughed, tipping his head back. Kate still

felt the sting of his grip on her arms, the red swollen marks that would likely become bruises. Aiden looked up at her, his eyes heavy with concern, the tears there betraying the rough facade he was portraying to Lord Evan. "Did he hurt you?" he asked in a soft voice.

She shook her head, lifting her chin as she stepped out of the gig on shaking legs. "Only a little."

Aiden's jaw clenched as he held Lord Evan in front of him. She shook with fear. How could he dare fight one of his masters? But had she heard Lord Evan call him *stepbrother*? She could hardly hear or think past her racing heart.

"What is happening here?" The deep and rather booming voice of her father came, rising above the hooves of his horse as they slowed upon the ground. She looked behind her, relieved to see her father astride his horse, approaching with command.

Lord Evan put on an expression of terror, cowering away from Aiden with a pointed finger. "This man, this *servant* in my home, has attempted to steal away with your daughter to Gretna Green. He planned to force her into an elopement."

Kate shook her head fast, her words freezing in her throat. Her father's anger mounted, reddening his cheeks as he looked at Aiden.

"I managed to stop him, your grace." Lord Evan bowed, a shaky smile of triumph on his lips.

"That is not true," Kate said, rushing toward her

father as he dismounted. "No, father, you must listen to me. It was Lord Evan that—"

"My son speaks the truth." A second voice pierced the clearing, a second horse approaching behind her father's—Lord Aveley's. The marquess dismounted, placing a gloved hand on the duke's shoulder. "My servant has been speaking of nothing else but his desire to marry your daughter. He seeks her fortune, you see."

Aiden exchanged a look with Kate, an honest denial in his eyes. He stepped closer to her, his voice lowered. "I am not merely their servant, though they treat me as such. Lord Aveley is my stepfather, and Evan my stepbrother."

As the revelation sunk in, Kate glanced eagerly at her father. Would he trust Aiden? How could he not? Aiden was clearly much more trustworthy than his sneering stepbrother and wicked stepfather. But the duke's gaze only hardened in Aiden's direction. "I will not believe a word from you after you attempted to deceive me, declaring yourself to be Lord Orsett."

"Papa!" Kate tried to pull her father's eyes back to her, but they remained fixed on Aiden.

"It is fortuitous indeed that Lord Evan was present to stop you."

She curled her hands into fists at her sides. "*Papa*!" He looked down at her, bewildered.

"For once, listen to me!" Kate's breathing came heavy, rasped, her heart pounding fast. "My word must be accounted for above that of a marquess, or his son. I am your daughter." She had his attention. "Lord Evan abducted me with the intent to elope. Aid—er— Mr. Notley came to my rescue."

Her father drew a deep breath, searching her eyes with suspicion. His voice was quiet when he spoke again. "How do you know this Mr. Notley?"

Aiden had moved closer, his eyes fixed on her when she turned around.

"He… he is a dear friend." Her voice shook with emotion. "He would never harm anyone. He rescued Freddy once, and now he has rescued me. Please believe me, Papa."

Lord Aveley scoffed, drawing her father's gaze. "My son would never treat a lady in such a manner. But my servant would."

Kate's father's eyes darted between Aiden and Lord Aveley. "Is it true? Is this your stepson?"

"No, of course not. He is my servant."

Aiden bowed to her father before speaking. "Your grace, if my word means anything to you, I would promise that, yes, I am Lord Aveley's stepson. I reside at Colborne Hall. I heard that Lord Evan planned to force a marriage with your daughter. I apologize for claiming a false identity, but it was the only way I could enter the ball in my attempt to protect her."

Kate watched her father's quizzical brow as he turned to Lord Aveley. "Why do you claim this man as your servant?"

"Well," the marquess stammered, "he does the

work of a servant. We cannot afford to staff many of them." He snapped his mouth shut, cursing under his breath. "What I mean to say is—"

"That is enough." Kate's father pulled her close, away from Aiden and the other men. "All of you must desert my property at once. My daughter's safety is of my greatest concern, and I do not trust one of you."

"Papa, no." Kate turned toward Aiden, but her father pulled her back. "You must believe me. Mr. Notley has done no harm."

"Come," her father said in a gruff voice, pulling her gently along toward the house. She stared at Aiden over her shoulder, apologizing with her eyes. Would she ever see him again? What would Lord Aveley do to him? Surely her father would never let her court him after what had happened that evening. Did Mr. Notley even desire to court her? He had never said as much. His actions that night could have simply been the result of his kindness. But she remembered that day in the woods, when he had said he was falling in love with her.

Her heart ached as her father pulled her far away from Aiden and far away from the woods. Freddy followed closely at her heels. When they reached the house, her father led her inside, leading her past the ballroom doors and toward his study. When they entered the small room, he closed the door, keeping her far away from any other of their guests that could have sinister intentions.

Her father sat down at the desk, putting his forehead in his hands. "I should have done more to protect you," he muttered.

"It is not your fault." Kate cradled her elbows, her heart rate just beginning to slow. For the first time that night, she remembered her right foot was bare and the hem of her dress was torn. "Aiden rescued me."

Her father's head jerked up, his eyes hard. "Aiden? You are familiar enough to use his Christian name?"

Kate lowered her eyes. "Yes. We have met on other occasions. It began when he rescued Freddy from the brook, then we met again, just to allow our dogs to play, and then again in town—"

He let out a long sigh. "How long have been having these secret meetings with Lord Aveley's stepson?"

"Not long. But long enough for me to know that he is a kind and honorable man."

"You haven't… developed an attachment to him, have you?"

Kate's legs shook beneath her. "Yes, Papa. I have. I care for him very much. But I know you will not approve of such a match. And I do not know if Mr. Notley still cares for me, and—"

"Oh, Kate." Her father's eyes lightened. "There is no question that he does."

She pressed her lips together, a smile pulling at them.

"I trust your word above Lord Aveley's or his sons, you must know."

Kate drew a quiet gasp. "You believe that Lord Evan is guilty? Against the word of the marquess?"

"I have never seen a more sincere face as Mr. Notley's." Her father's gaze sparked with amusement. "Especially regarding his love for you. I have never wished anything but happiness upon you. But I have been selfish desiring a prestigious match for you. I should have desired an honorable man for you above all else. And I see you have found one."

Tears stung her eyes anew, joyful ones that brought a smile to her cheeks.

Her mother burst through the door, gasping as her eyes fell on Kate. She bustled forward in her layered skirts, throwing her arms around Kate. "Oh, I thought I had lost you forever!" She squeezed Kate before pulling back to grip her cheeks between her hands. She turned to her husband. "I have sent all the guests home. I could not bear the thought of any other wicked men abducting Katherine."

"There will be no more of that, I assure you. Lord Aveley and his son will be brought to trial for what they have done. Not to worry."

Kate pressed a hand to her chest. "Papa, what will Mr. Notley do? Where will he live?"

He rubbed his jaw. "Would you like to marry him? If that is so, Silverbard is unoccupied at present. You ought to practice managing the estate before it is yours entirely. I trust Mr. Notley will be a worthy partner for you. He has saved you from a life of unhappiness with that dreadful Lord Evan, a debt to which I could never repay him."

Kate blinked, her ears pounding with her pulse. The clock on the wall of the study began its loud chiming, the two clock hands coming together after twelve hours of being apart. Midnight.

"Who is Mr. Notley?" Kate's mother said, her voice astonished. "Is he the man that rescued you?" She gripped Kate's hands. "Is he titled? How are his connections?"

Kate exchanged a glance with her father. "His familial connections are rather atrocious, and he has no title or wealth to speak of." She smiled, her heart soaring. "But he is kind."

"Kind?" Her mother's lips turned down in a grimace. "Is that all?"

No. Kate could list dozens of things that Aiden possessed that were greater than connections or wealth or prestige. What had she done to deserve so much? He was a greater prize than any dowry or estate. The clock still chimed behind her, loud and vibrating.

"Oh, why do you still have that odious clock?" Kate's mother covered her ears as the final chimes of the midnight hour sounded, striking in Kate's heart with hope. Would she really be allowed to court Aiden? She had never thought it possible. But a small part of her still doubted. Would he still want her even after she had hurt him—lied to him about her identity?

"Thank you, Papa." She stepped away from her

mother to grip her father's hand. "But Mr. Notley has not made an offer to me. I deceived him." She shook her head. "I pretended to be my lady's maid."

The eyes of both her parents rounded in shock. "Then he cannot possibly be a fortune hunter," her father said, a deep chuckle catching in his throat.

"He is not." Kate smiled.

"I am glad to hear it, knowing how much you despise them." He winked. "I could certainly see his feelings for you were genuine. But not to worry," he yawned, stretching his arms overhead as he reclined in his chair. "I expect he will be here tomorrow, begging my permission to marry you. In the meantime, I will ensure no harm comes upon him at the hands of his stepfather and stepbrothers. They will have a visit from the constable at first light."

Kate didn't want to wait until the next day to see Aiden. She didn't doubt his ability to defend himself from his relatives, but she wanted to ensure his safety as he had ensured hers that night. She wanted to explain her deception to him, to confess her feelings to him, to discover if he felt the same.

There was a knock on the door of the study, pulling Kate from her thoughts.

"Enter," her father said.

The door opened at the hands of a footman. Standing beside him, his jacket torn and his trousers streaked in dirt, his face ruddy and his hair falling in dark tangles on his forehead, was Aiden. His eyes, light brown, captured her gaze, a smile shining through them, though his mouth remained serious.

He bowed, first to her father, then her mother. "Your grace," he addressed the duke, "Forgive my intrusion, but—"

"It is no intrusion." Her father stood, a gleam of joy in his eyes that seemed to surprise Aiden. "Come in. I will allow you a private audience with my daughter."

Aiden's face did not conceal emotion well. He looked altogether shocked, pleased, and far too endearing to be fair. Kate's heart galloped as he entered.

She stood, catching her mother's reluctant eye as both she and Kate's father exited the study. Kate followed Aiden's eyes as they settled on the door handle, watching it turn as the door closed. The moment it did, he walked forward, taking both of her hands in his. "Kate," he whispered, tipping his head close. "Are you well? Are you hurt? Please, tell me honestly."

A pang of guilt hit her. "You have good reason to doubt my honesty. I should not have pretended to be a maid."

He touched her cheek, his hand warm and strong and safe. "I am glad you did. I very well could have been a conniving fortune hunter." A whisper of a grin touched his lips. "I hope if you ever meet another man in the woods you will tell him you are a maid as well. It was a wise decision, and I do not blame you for it." There was a certain sadness in his voice, hanging on his words with a weight she wanted to erase.

"Would you find yourself… envious if I found another man in the woods?"

He seemed surprised by the question, but then the heaviness reached his eyes. "Yes. Very much." Silence hung between him, his fingers still resting on her face, tracing over her cheek and jaw. He tucked a strand of hair behind her ear, his fingertips grazing her neck as he dropped his hand. "I would be tempted to throw him in the brook, in fact. Or feed his hand to Freddy."

She giggled, covering her mouth. She had been hiding her smile, repressing her joy.

He stared at her with piqued curiosity, his own sadness still reflected in his features. "But it does not matter, Kate. Does it?" His voice turned sad. "I could never give you the connections your father desires for you. I'm a tradesman. I am a cordwainer's apprentice." He dug through the bag he wore across his body, withdrawing a small, gold satin slipper.

She felt keenly the cold floor beneath her toes.

Aiden's brows drew together, his mouth a tight line. "You lost this when Evan abducted you. It's how Freddy and I discovered your location. I recognized it as yours because I made it."

"You made it?" she breathed, staring at the beautiful shoe. Her heart pounded. "Th-thank you. But is this the only reason you have come? To return the shoe to me?"

He hesitated, his eyes fixed unwaveringly on hers. Three beats of silence passed between them before he spoke. "No."

"No?"

He dropped the slipper to the floor and stepped close to her once again, taking her hand in his. He took several deep breaths and swallowed, his throat rising and falling along with his chest. "I—I also came to say—to tell you…" He exhaled sharply, squeezing his eyes shut. In a flash, his eyes opened, meeting hers with an intensity she had never seen before. "I love you." The softness of his voice threaded into her heart, squeezing and pounding and filling it with joy. "I love you, Kate. I would not care if you were a lady's maid, or a dairy maid, or a scullery maid." He swiped away the tear that slipped from her eye.

"I love you, too," she whispered, her skin tingling from his touch. Emotion choked her, joy and peace overcoming all the dread and uncertainty she had felt earlier that evening. All she could see and feel were Aiden and his beautiful eyes and smile and words. "I love you more than Freddy loves you, which is quite a lot."

He smiled, cupping her face in his hands. His eyes lowered to her lips, his head tipping closer. He met her eyes again, his expression growing serious. "If I could somehow convince your father to allow it, would you honor me by accepting my proposal of marriage? I can't imagine my life without you, Kate."

She smiled. "My father has already expressed his approval."

Aiden's eyes widened, hope seizing his expression. "Truly? But I have nothing to give you."

She shook her head. "That is not true. You have given me everything I could ever want."

His mouth stretched into a smile, and he pressed his lips to her forehead. Taking her face gently between his hands, he pulled her close. His lips brushed over hers, soft and gentle, like the sweep of a bird's wings. She sighed, and he deepened their kiss, threading his fingers through her hair. She had never felt more loved, more happy or secure in her life. She leaned into him, kissing him in return, savoring their brief embrace.

He pulled back, staring into her eyes. "You never did give me an answer."

"You kissed me before I could," she teased, and he kissed her lips one more time. When she could breathe again, she gave him the answer she never thought she would be allowed to give. "Yes." She laughed, and so did he, their joy too much to be kept contained by mere smiles. He scooped her slipper up from off the ground, pulling out her chair for her to sit.

Kneeling before her, he held out the slipper. She extended her leg, allowing him to slip the shoe onto her stockinged foot before he pulled her up and into his arms.

"Shall I make Freddy my groomsman?" he asked. "It would be a reward for his assistance in rescuing you this evening."

She laughed, enjoying the warmth of his arms around her. She rested her head against his chest, closing her eyes as he pressed a kiss into her hair. "He would like that very much."

Kate could think of nothing she would like more than to marry Aiden, to live the rest of her life with him. The fears she had felt at the idea of managing Silverbard alone had fled, replaced with the assurance of the man at her side. His laugh rumbled against her.

Against all odds, the original wishes of her father, and the doubts of her mind, she would marry Aiden Notley. Her heart soared. And she was certain they would live—a struggling apprentice and a reluctant heiress—quite happily ever after.

# Other Books in the Series

## Once Upon a Regency

THE FAIREST HEART

by Heather Chapman

THE MIDNIGHT HEIRESS

by Ashtyn Newbold

SPUN OF GOLD

by Jen Geigle Johnson

BEAUTY'S ROSE

by Rebecca J. Greenwood

AWAKE AT WIDMORE MANOR

by Jessilyn Stewart Peaslee

# About the Author

Ashtyn Newbold grew up with a love of stories. When she discovered chick flicks and Jane Austen books in high school, she learned she was a sucker for romantic ones. When not indulging in sweet romantic comedies and regency period novels (and cookies), she writes romantic stories of her own across several genres. Ashtyn also enjoys baking, singing, sewing, and anything that involves creativity and imagination.

Made in the USA
Middletown, DE
21 August 2020